PAT

BOOK ONE

BY L.T. RYAN

Affliction Z: Patient Zero

(Book One)

L.T. Ryan

PUBLISHED BY:
L.T. Ryan

ISBN-13: 978-1483997186
ISBN-10: 1483997189

Feedback on this book can be sent to:
Ltryan70@gmail.com

Or on the web:
http://LTRyan.com
http://www.afflictionz.com
http://www.facebook.com/AfflictionZSeries

Chapter 1

Sean Ryder prepared himself for what would end up being the final HALO jump of his career. He clung tightly to the yellow length of cord that kept him from being swept out of the rear of the C-160. No more than thirty feet from where he stood was the platform, lowered and ready for the men to jump. A dozen men lined up, ready to free fall for twenty thousand feet or more before deploying their chutes. Their calls of bravado steadied the men in the face of danger. Anything could go wrong. It rarely did, but the possibility was there and it preyed on the minds of each man.

From twenty-five thousand feet in the air, the Earth looked like scaled scenery that might have been used in an old movie. But Sean didn't see the ground. None of the men did, not tonight. The tops of dull gray clouds flew by a few thousand feet below the plane. Once in a while, there was a break in the cloud cover and Sean saw glimpses of darkened Earth. Blackness left behind by a sun that set five hours ago, its charred remains stretching across the landscape.

The SEALs made their jumps, one by one, in quick succession, with no hesitation, no fear, no bullshit. They were warriors in every sense of the word.

SEALs were like that, thought Sean.

He turned to his partner, Jules Hoover, and said, "We're up."

Jules winked and headed for the platform.

They had to move, and both men knew it. Waiting much longer would put them further away from the team they were attached to. The SEALs wouldn't wait around long, if at all. Not in hostile territory. Not for a couple of Air Force Pararescuemen, otherwise known as PJs.

In a flash, Jules took off down the ramp and dove head first, arms out, legs spread wide. When Sean reached the ledge, Jules had disappeared into the night sky.

"These things we do, that others may live," Sean said to himself. The PJ motto. He repeated it to himself at the start of every mission, every time he had to use deadly force against another human being, and every time he risked his life to save another.

He reached into his top pocket, pulled out a photograph. He stared at the two smiling faces, both framed by long brown hair. He kissed the image of his wife, Kathy, did the same to the image of his daughter, Emma. He thought back to the words Emma whispered to him right before he left for this mission.

Please stay safe, Daddy.

Sean smiled. At four years old, his daughter had no idea what he did. She knew he was in the Air Force and that his job involved saving people. He figured that she picked up on some of Kathy's anxiety of his missions, and that's why she insisted that he stay safe.

Knowing that his window to jump was closing, Sean took one last look at the photo, whispered, "I'll be home soon, ladies," and tucked the picture away in a spot he knew it would remain safe. From that point on, he had to focus on his job. He compartmentalized the two women in his life, tucked them away in a spot where he knew they were there, but his thoughts of them wouldn't interfere with the job he had to do. It was something he learned to do long ago. It kept him, and those around him, alive.

No matter how many times he'd jumped, he'd never managed to get rid of the anxious feelings that preceded plummeting to the Earth at terminal velocity. His stomach knotted, sweat dripped profusely, his chest tightened, his lungs constricted. But the panic and anxiety never stopped him. Not tonight. Not any night. Sean knew that extended periods of anxiety could cause hypoxia, so he allowed himself a panic window of fifteen seconds. Ten before the jump, five after.

He traveled down the platform, his movements silent against the roar of the rushing wind. He propelled himself off the ledge, head first, arms out, feet wide. Then gravity took over and he repositioned himself to travel like a bullet.

The first few moments of a jump were always terrifying. Questions raced through Sean's mind. They were the same every time. *What if I fail to maintain control of my body? What if atmospheric conditions blow me off course and into enemy hands? What if my chute doesn't open? What if my backup fails to deploy in time?* The questions passed through him like grains of sand through a child's fingers. He continued toward the Earth, and the powerful upper level winds that Sean knifed through carried his doubts away, like dust in a sandstorm.

With terminal velocity achieved, Sean let his training and instincts take over. By this point in his career, he had enough jumps to his credit that the process was as close to automatic as it could get. His only concerns were how far he'd have to travel to rejoin the group, and whether or not the journey would be wrought with danger. He knew that Jules would be close by and the man would wait for Sean to rendezvous with him before moving on. Together, they could take on a dozen regular men and half a dozen soldiers, so long as they didn't have the same type of training.

At twenty-five hundred feet, Sean pulled his ripcord. Nothing happened. The first twinges of panic surfaced and were subsequently beaten away by Sean's extensive training and preparation. He deployed his reserve and prepared for the worst. His reserve parachute opened and he felt his body jerk to a crawl. At least that was how it felt after plummeting at a speed of over one hundred and twenty miles per hour.

Floating through the air afforded Sean a chance to scan the area for other members of the team. Using a pair of night vision goggles, he located what he assumed was Jules's parachute. A moment later, he saw the grainy dark green outline of his partner, and the first leg of his journey was confirmed. Sean kept his eyes on his partner's location until he hit the ground. The landing wasn't as rough as he had expected it to be. It wasn't great, either, but he managed to get up and walk away, and for Sean, that constituted a successful jump.

Adrenaline streamed through his body, pumping with every rapid beat of his heart. He gathered up his parachute then headed in the direction of Jules's landing spot. He had to remind himself to proceed with extreme caution. No immediate danger had been expected, but he knew they wouldn't be in the area if there wasn't a damn good reason. Rarely did they get this far into a mission without details about where they were going and what they would do once they arrived. Yet, here they were, in the wilds of southern Nigeria, a few miles north of the snaking Niger River, and no one could tell him anything other than *jump*.

Sean reached Jules's landing spot and found his partner crouching low, facing the opposite direction. He dropped to his stomach, crawled toward Jules.

"Something's out there," Jules said.

"What?" Sean said.

"Not sure. I heard it. Saw it for a second. It rushed in, then back out."

"Animal?"

"Bi-pedal, man. It ran in on two feet, then took off."

"You don't think it was Bates or Schmitty messing with you?"

Jules shrugged and appeared to contemplate the question. On the half dozen or so missions they'd run with this platoon, Bates and Schmitty always came up with a way to screw with Jules. Last time they'd been attached, the two guys got Jules piss drunk on tequila. When he passed out, they stuck him in an emergency raft and dragged him a quarter mile out into the Caspian Sea. Sean got the call at daybreak and had to figure out how to get his partner back to land.

"C'mon, forget about it" Sean said. "We need to catch up with them. I've got no idea where we're heading."

"Me either," Jules said. He hopped to his feet, started moving.

Sean reequipped his night vision then caught up to his partner. They walked side by side, both of them scanning the area in front of them and to the sides, and occasionally behind. Their MP7s moved with their eyes, ready to eliminate any threats.

"Did you see them land?" Sean asked in a hushed voice.

"Yeah," Jules replied. "They were a good half-mile away. Guess we took more wind shear than they did."

Sean felt like he'd managed to land pretty close to his target. Of course, an accurate gauge of distance was harder from five miles in the air, especially in the dark. His initial trajectory from the plane could have been off an inch or two and that would have made a big difference.

Sean heard a scattering sound to his right. He twisted his head and stared into the thick vegetation. He looked up and down, left and right, focusing on one six-foot section at a time. The branches stood out, almost white, in the greenish hue of the goggles. The sound stopped almost as soon as it began. Sean decided to ignore it and continue on.

Probably wildlife.

"Think they're waiting?" Jules said.

"No," Sean said. "Call 'em and tell them to stop or at least slow down. I don't want them to get too far ahead."

"Okay," Jules said.

Sean heard another sound, again to his right. Footsteps scurrying across the ground, close by, then retreating. He spun to his right, heard Jules do the same.

"What the frig?" Jules said.

Sean said nothing as he scanned the area, looking for any sign of what made the noise.

"Did you see that, Sean?"

"See what?"

"That… thing?"

"I didn't see anything."

But was that the truth? Sean thought through the sequence of events. He'd heard the sound approach and turned as whatever had created the noise retreated into the brush. He had scanned a large area of bushes and trees. He'd seen it. A human figure had ducked in between two bushes.

Jules approached the area, slowly and cautiously.

"What're you doing?" Sean said. He remained rooted to the same spot.

"I want to know what that is," Jules called back.

"Screw it, man. It's gone and we need to catch up to Turk and the others. Keep your eyes open and stay alert."

Jules stood in place, facing the thick vegetation. His elbows were tight to his side. His arms out, hidden from Sean's view by Jules's torso. He pivoted left to right. Sean saw the barrel of the man's H&K MP7 poke out on the side.

"Jules," Sean said, maybe a notch too loud. "Let's move."

"All right," Jules said, turning. "Damn mind playing tricks on me. Swore I saw eyes reflecting from in there."

Sean chuckled, managing to find something humorous in the situation. He imagined them being stalked by a pack of feral cats.

Ten pounds of pure terror.

A scream that could rival that of a banshee erupted from within the bushes. Time slowed down. Sean saw Jules twist around. The man's arms went up into a protective gesture. The weapon in his hands rose to a spot in front of his face to deflect a blow. Jules's body bowed back at his knees. He looked like he was trying to win a limbo competition, only the bar was coming after him.

Sean reacted before his mind could fully process the sight of a naked human, or humanoid, rushing toward him. Its mouth hung wide open, strands of saliva connected between upper and lower teeth. Its eyes seemed to glow. Sean lifted his pistol into the air. It was his only defense, as he hadn't yet removed his MP7. He squeezed off three shots. Each one hit dead center. The man that approached jerked back at first, then staggered backward. It released another furious howl. Pain? Anger? Then it began another approach.

"What the...?" Sean said. Unfortunately, his brain had caught up and was busy trying to make sense of what had happened. Even a man high on PCP would have had more of a reaction than this guy had after three 9mm bullets to the chest. He should be on the ground sucking in his dying breaths, yet here he was, standing and looking even more pissed off.

Sean aimed, fired two more rounds. One hit the man in the stomach and the guy bowed forward. The other shot hit him in his shoulder, and the man jerked back to the left, his body twisting at the waist.

Sean cursed himself for allowing his nerves to affect his aim. He dropped to one knee in an effort to steady himself. The man was now close enough that Sean had to make his next shot count, or it might be his last.

The guy straightened, dropped his head back. He released a scream that drowned out the ambient sounds of the night. It started low and sounded guttural. *Primal*. Then it became high and shrill. The sound was deafening, and Sean wondered if maybe it was an attempt to call another person to his position.

Sean lifted his weapon and took aim, but before he could squeeze the trigger, the man sprinted toward him, moving faster than he'd ever seen a human run. The next thing he knew, the guy was right in front of him, arms out and back at the elbows, fingers curled up like claws, mouth open and teeth glinting in the moonlight. The guy carried the smell of rotten and decaying flesh and human waste. Blood leaked from the bullet holes that riddled the man's body. He breathed heavily, wheezing with each inhale and exhale.

This was no man.

The roar of three-burst semi-automatic gunfire erupted from behind the man. The bullets appeared to hit him in the mid to upper back, because the guy stopped and his stomach extended out while his shoulders pulled back. His open, vicious mouth contorted in a pained expression. Another burst of gunfire tore through the night and ripped through the man's head, tearing a good chunk of the right side off. Blood and bone and brain hovered in the air, and then rained to the ground.

Sean fell back and rolled out of the way. He lay flat on his stomach and aimed at the *being*, which still stood, though appeared lifeless. At last, it fell forward, the remains of its face hitting the packed earth, Jules standing a foot behind the space it had occupied.

"What the fuck was that?" Sean yelled.

Jules shook his head, said nothing.

Sean got to his feet, walked around the body on the ground. He noticed Jules standing still, mouth open, eyes glassy and focused on the corpse on the ground.

"Jules?" Sean said.

His partner said nothing in return. He continued to stare at the body.

Sean lifted his goggles and shone a light on the body on the ground. It was pale, almost blue. Half of its face was exposed. An open mouth revealed red gums and dirty, yellow-and-brown teeth. Deep-purple circles rimmed its eyes. Dark bruises littered its upper back and thighs. Sean wanted to see its stomach, but decided against touching the remains. The fear, he thought, was irrational, but he knew he had every right to trust his instincts.

Sean's radio clicked on, and through a faint trace of static, a deep voice spoke. "Ryder, Jules? Come in." It was Turk, the SEAL team leader.

"Ryder," Sean said.

"What are you two clowns doing back there? We heard gunfire."

"That was us. We're okay," Sean said.

"Care to tell me what happened?" Turk asked.

Sean looked at Jules, who appeared to have regained some sense. Jules shook his head and in a hushed tone said, "Don't tell them."

Sean licked his lips and pressed the transmit button on his radio. "Wild boar or some shit."

"Wild boar?" Turk said. "That was a hell of a lot of gunfire for a friggin' pig, Ryder."

"Yeah," Sean said. "We thought there were more behind the bushes."

"Whatever," Turk said. "You two need to hustle and get your asses over here. I'm serious, double time it. I got no idea who's out here waiting for us, but I do know that you two numb nuts alerted them to our presence. Out."

Sean reattached his radio to his belt. "Not who," he muttered. "What." He bumped into Jules's shoulder and began walking away from the lifeless body on the ground, hoping to forget about the encounter.

"Turk's right," Jules said.

Sean waited for him to continue, but when Jules said nothing else, Sean said, "How's that?"

Jules turned his head ninety degrees and looked at Sean. He, too, had removed his goggles. His dark brown eyes reflected the moon as tiny white circles. "He ain't got no idea what's out here. We've seen it, and we ain't got a clue."

Sean said nothing. He started walking and picked up the pace once they were a few yards away. He wanted to put as much distance between himself and the body of that *thing* as he could. If they encountered another one, he didn't want to be alone. And the SEALs wouldn't wait all night.

Chapter 2

They moved quickly, quietly, deliberately. Their eyes scanned the territory in front of them and behind them, non-stop. Sean maintained radio silence, a precaution in the event that their gunfire had alerted someone of their presence.

Sean couldn't be sure, but he thought he heard howls that sounded more human than animal. Feral humans, he thought. Could that be what that *thing* was?

It took fifteen minutes for Sean and Jules to reach the SEAL team, which indicated to Sean that the SEALs had held position after they heard the attack.

Sean wanted to locate Turk so he could avoid him. He knew the man would again ask what happened. If Sean lied a second time, it would show on his face. Keeping Jules away from Turk was also a high priority because he appeared to still be on edge over the situation. Every couple hundred feet or so during their journey, Jules would mutter something to the effect of, "What the frig was that thing? Never seen no man take that kind of damage and keep moving." Sean had to constantly remind his partner to keep quiet in case there were more of those *things* around.

Jules's question and observation were legit, as far as Sean was concerned. He'd completed PJ training over ten years ago. During that time, he'd been in some of the worst places imaginable. He'd seen people wounded in any of a hundred different ways. He'd had to use deadly force on a number of occasions in an effort to complete a mission.

Through it all, he'd never seen someone handle a catastrophic injury and keep on coming. Perhaps, as he guessed, they weren't dealing with a someone. But what, then? An alien? He chuckled at the thought.

Jules turned his head. His thick eyebrows were furrowed over his dark eyes. "What the frig are you laughing about?"

Sean shrugged, brushed off Jules's question. Not because he wanted to ignore the man, though. He had locked eyes with Turk, and the SEAL was crossing camp, heading in their direction.

Turk was one of the most intimidating men Sean had ever been around. It wasn't only his physical traits. All SEALs were built and fast and tough. Turk had something else about him. The guy had close to twenty years in the Navy, almost all of them as a SEAL. Two of those years had been spent in a dirt hole four foot wide and ten foot deep, crisscrossed iron bars at the top, trapping him inside. One day, his captors made a mistake and forgot to lock down the gate atop the hole. According to Turk, he waited an hour or so for the sun to set, and then scaled the muddy walls. He said he left one of his captors alive, but only after removing the man's genitals and forcing him to eat them. A warning, he said, that they should never fuck with SEALs. Turk was legendary within the SEAL community. Hell, he was legendary in the Special Forces community. It always gave Sean a sense of calm when Turk was in charge of a mission.

"What's wrong with him?" Turk said, nodding at Jules.

Sean hesitated. If he said the wrong thing, Turk would know he was bullshitting him. And if he took too long to answer, Turk would grow suspicious. More so than he appeared to be.

"Well?" Turk said. "Your tongues tired from making out on the way over here?"

A few members of the SEAL team turned to look. Sean saw grins plastered on their faces. He knew that if he was going to tell Turk what happened, the two of them should step away from the camp. It was as much to prevent rumors of Sean's impending lunacy as it was to prevent panic among the ranks.

"Turk," Sean said. "Let's talk over there." He pointed to a distant spot.

"All right," Turk said. "What about him?" He gestured toward Jules again.

Sean looked at his partner. The man looked lost and Sean figured that Jules would be better off staying behind.

"He'll wait here," Sean said.

They walked in silence for fifty yards. Sean remained alert. He'd armed himself with his H&K MP7 and affixed the suppressor. The bullets weren't any stronger than his 9mm, but he could fire in a semi-automatic burst of three rounds, giving him a greater chance of incapacitating his target.

"What are you so sketchy about, Ryder?" Turk asked.

"Turk," Sean said, "it wasn't a boar."

"No shit."

Sean was glad he didn't attempt to lie to the man.

"We were attacked," Sean said.

"Why didn't you say so?" Turk said.

"In case we lost integrity of our communications. I didn't want to endanger you. We were passing through an area that you guys hadn't. As far as they knew, Jules and I were alone."

Turk nodded. "Okay, go on."

Sean took a deep breath, looked up at the thinly veiled moon, then exhaled. "It came out of the bushes."

"It?" Turk crossed his arms and leaned back.

"You heard all the shots, yeah?"

Turk nodded.

"That was for one, uh, man," Sean said.

"Eleven frickin' shots?" Turk widened his stance as he took a step back.

Sean nodded. The story sounded better in his head, believable. But as the words left his mouth, he knew that he'd have a hard time convincing Turk of what happened.

"I'm calling bullshit. You guys gotta be better shots than that. I don't care if you are Air Force." He paused and grinned momentarily over his jab at Sean. "I want to see the damn body."

"Turk," Sean said. "You don't want to do that. There's more I have to tell—"

Turk had already turned and was jogging toward camp. He stopped and yelled for two of the men to meet him, then he turned back toward Sean. "C'mon, Ryder. You're taking us to the body."

Sean wondered what the hell he'd gotten himself into.

"Jules going to accompany us?" Turk asked.

Sean shook his head. No way he'd lead Jules back down that path. The guy might go insane by the time they made it back to camp.

"You remember where you left the body?" Turk asked.

"Yeah," Sean replied. "I remember."

They started back in the direction of the attack. Sean walked fast, having already been through the territory and feeling more comfortable about his chances with three members of SEAL Team 8 surrounding him. If another one of those *things* attacked, the men would be on it like white on rice. They'd fill it so full of holes it wouldn't have a chance to reach them.

They found the location where the thing had attacked, but the body was gone.

"What?" Turk asked, likely wondering why Sean had stopped.

"I don't understand," Sean said. "It was here. We left the body where it fell."

"You sure this is the right spot?" Turk said.

Sean nodded. He panned his flashlight on the ground, stopped when spent shells glinted in the light.

"Those are proof," Sean said. "This is where it happened."

"Blood," Spencer said. "Pool of it here. It looks like your guy was dragged into the brush over there." He shone his light in a zigzag pattern against the dense vegetation.

"Don't do that," Sean said.

Turk said, "So there was more than one guy, huh Ry—"

A scream erupted from beyond the trail of blood. "*Whoooo-aaaaaaah*." Low to high, guttural and primal.

"The hell was that?" Turk said.

A similar-sounding scream ripped through the still night from the opposite direction, maybe a hundred yards or so from where they stood. The ambient sounds of nature disappeared, giving way to the echo of the screams.

"We need to move," Sean said. He hadn't had time to allow fear to invade his psyche at the time of the earlier attack. It was kill or die at that time. But now, after knowing what those *things* were capable of, and the set of shrieks indicating that he and the SEALs weren't alone, he found himself wishing that he and Jules hadn't been called upon for this mission. What was the mission? Was this the reason why they hadn't been told why they were out here? Someone didn't have the balls to tell them they were dealing with some kind of mutated sub-human species?

The deafening silence was interrupted by the sound of a twig snapping, perhaps under the pale foot of one of those beings. Sean prepared himself for the next shrill scream, or worse, another one of those *things* to rush at them from behind the veil of darkness. If he weren't clutching his weapon so tightly, he was positive his hands would be shaking uncontrollably.

Turk remained motionless. His eyes were closed, his head tilted back. An attempt to tune himself to the environment, Sean presumed. He figured that after two years in a muddy hole, nothing would be entirely frightening anymore. No situation too dangerous. Death would pass by with a wink and a smile, knowing it had been bested once already.

"Anyone else smelling that?" Turk said, his voice low so as not to be heard too far from their position.

"That's the way it... he smelled," Sean said. "It looked, I don't know, rotten, and covered in shit."

"Got the shit part right," Turk said.

They remained in the same spot for another five minutes. There were no more screams, no twigs snapping. The smell faded, or perhaps they had become used to it.

"Let's get outta here," Turk said. "Ryder, you cover the back. I'll be point. You two watch the side. Move slow and then haul ass on my command."

Sean had been too preoccupied with the situation to check his watch before they left camp. He wasn't sure how long it took them to reach the spot of the attack, but he estimated their return at less than eight minutes. They walked slowly at first, every step a deliberate attempt to not be noticed and to notice anything that might be watching them. After a couple hundred yards, they increased their pace to a run.

When they reached the camp, Sean found Jules sitting alone. He dropped his gear and sat down next to his partner.

"How'd it go?" Jules asked. "What'd they do with the body?"

Sean contemplated his answer for a minute. Lying would be the best option if he were partnered with any other PJ. But he couldn't lie to Jules, the man would see right through him. He had to be straight with the man.

"Body was gone," Sean replied.

Jules turned his head and swallowed hard. "What d'ya mean? Missing?"

Sean hiked his shoulders an inch, shook his head. "It was gone, man. Shells on the ground. Pool of blood where it collapsed. There was a trail of blood that led into the brush where it had come out from."

"You think it got back up?"

"Nah," Sean said. "You saw its head. It looked like the body was dragged away."

"There's more." A statement, not a question.

Sean nodded. "Heard one of those howls from inside the brush. Close. Then another one from the opposite side, but further away. If you asked me, I'd say it was two more of them, and they were communicating." He placed his palm on the ground and kicked his legs out from under himself. "And the smell, man. That rotten, shit-stained smell was still there."

"What'd Turk say?" Jules turned his head slightly and looked at Sean out of the corner of his left eye, presumably in an attempt to gauge Sean's reaction to the question.

Sean didn't hesitate with his response. "I think he thinks I'm full of it. But he sure as hell was cautious when we started back."

Jules nodded and said nothing.

"Wish we'd found that body. Maybe we'd be getting out of here if we had."

"You think that's why we're out here? Those *things*?"

"I don't know, man. I don't know." Sean hopped up. "Why don't you get some sleep, Jules? I'll watch out for a while then we'll switch."

"They'll have someone watching." Jules lifted his chin and nodded toward the SEALs.

"They'll be watching their own asses if those *things* show up here. We gotta watch our own."

Chapter 3

Turk lay on the packed ground with nothing but a dull green sheet between him and the dirt. He interlaced his fingers behind his head and crossed his feet at the ankles. A hill jutted up from the ground a half-mile away, silhouetted by the rising moon, which was wide and oval and red. Turk watched the moon rise above the hill and ascend into the sky, turning small and circular and white. In less than ten minutes the orb shrunk to a tenth of the size it had been when he first saw it.

It was bright enough that Turk didn't need to use his flashlight to see the bodies that lay on the ground around the campsite. He easily spotted the dark outlines of his two men that were on patrol. They circled the site, keeping watch for whatever was out there. The moon also provided enough light that he was able to make out the shapes of shrubs dotting the hillside. He couldn't see them with any detail. He was too far away and it was too dark for that. But, he could tell they were there.

However, when one of the shrubs started moving toward the ridgeline, Turk became nervous. He got up and grabbed his SIG and his MP7. He held the former in his hand and strapped the latter across his chest. He reached into his bag and grabbed his night vision goggles and placed them on top of his head. Creating as little sound as possible, he crept in between and around his men, trying not to disturb them.

Ruiz turned to face Turk as he approached the outer perimeter of camp.

"What's up, T?" Ruiz said.

"Going to check something out. Nothing to be alarmed about. I'm not going far, and I'll radio in if something's wrong."

"You got it, Chief," Ruiz said, turning away and returning to his duties.

Almost twenty years in and Turk was rate capped at Chief. He'd never be a Senior Chief, or a Master Chief. Although, there were some who told him he was asshole enough to be either. But if Turk wanted to advance any further, he'd have to change rates. Hell with that, Turk thought.

Twenty yards away from camp, he donned his night vision goggles and began to scan the landscape. It was then that he realized the hillside had no shrubs on it. They were people, and they were on the move. Their movements carried them away from the campsite, so for now, Turk intended only to watch them. He crouched low and scanned the hillside. There were at least two dozen of them and they all walked up the hill, at an angle, to their left. Their gait was odd, and they seemed to move slowly. Turk thought it appeared as though some of them were dragging a leg, or maybe had trouble lifting both feet off the ground.

Turk worked his eyes up and down the hill in a zigzag pattern, ensuring he didn't miss a straggler. The people stopped walking once they reached the hilltop. They didn't bunch up tightly, but they did form a gathering. Their heads dropped back. They seemed to be looking up at the moon. Through the night vision goggles, they looked pale, and their eyes either dark as coal or completely translucent.

Turk had to remind himself to keep his eyes moving and not remain focused on the group at the top of the hill. He scanned the hillside and saw no more bodies moving. He returned his gaze to the group, then looked to the right of them. Another group had gathered at the far end of the hilltop, and had begun moving toward the people in the middle. Turk then looked toward the left side of the hill. There he saw dozens of them lined up in single file, moving slowly toward the middle of the hill.

What were they doing?

They didn't appear to be armed, although Turk couldn't be sure without seeing them up close. They could have side arms hidden underneath their clothes. Turk realized that their clothes were odd. It didn't matter whether they took the form of a man or a woman, they all appeared to be wearing gowns. Not robes, like you might see in certain areas of this continent. They were dressed in gowns that Turk could only compare to hospital gowns.

Turk wanted to get a better look. He had to determine the real reason for SEAL Team 8 being in Nigeria that night. He thought it over for a minute, decided to ascend the hill. He stayed low and moved slow. He didn't climb straight up, instead he used a left-to-right pattern, choosing to head more toward the left each pass so that he would come up a hundred yards or so away from the group. Since they appeared to not be carrying rifles, that would be far enough away that their aim with handguns would be somewhat compromised.

The entire time he climbed, Turk kept his eyes on the group, whether he was moving toward them or away from them. As the walkers met with the group in the middle, their heads inevitably turned upward to stare at the moon. Turk stopped to get another look at the sight. It appeared that they did not blink. They stood, stock still, staring up at a big hunk of glowing space rock. The spectacle struck Turk as odd. He decided to continue moving upward to get a better look.

He didn't take two steps before people on the outer edge of the formation atop the hill began turning around. Turk froze in place, held his breath. He watched the men and women shuffle in a semi-circle, facing his direction. He exhaled slow and low, then crouched when they continued turning around. Fifteen seconds later, they all faced the opposite direction and began traversing down the hill. Turk waited half a minute, then began moving, this time taking a line straight to the ridge. He had no idea what was on the other side, and didn't want to lose sight of the crowd of people.

It took a few minutes for Turk to reach the top. When he did, he lowered himself to his stomach and crawled the few remaining feet to the ridgeline. As he poked his head over, he saw that the hillside was barren. The people had already reached the bottom of the hill and now walked away from Turk and into a valley. A dozen or so split off to the left and slipped into a growth of bushes. There were a few stragglers that appeared to drop to their knees and lean over something placed on the ground. Turk couldn't make out what, though. It appeared to be another shape on the landscape. Eventually, the people rose and joined the others in the bushes.

The rest of the people converged on a central spot directly below Turk. As the group appeared to thin out, Turk realized that, one by one, they disappeared into a black hole, an entrance.

To what, though?

Turk wasn't sure, but he felt certain that whatever or wherever the hole led to, it was the reason he, his men, and the two PJs were in Nigeria.

The last person slipped into the hole, and the landscape below him became still. In fact, he felt it was too still. There was no sound at all, no rodents or insects or birds.

Turk began to slide backward in preparation to return to camp when he saw four more bodies approaching from the left. He flattened his body, held his breath. He worked his hands underneath his chest to grip his MP7 in case the group noticed him.

They didn't though. They walked right past him, then, in the same spot as all the others, descended the hill. Turk decided not to resume position atop the hill to investigate the smaller group any further.

He made his way back to camp and managed to get an hour of sleep.

Chapter 4

Sean awoke to someone kicking the bottom of his boots. He squinted his eyes open and instinctively brought his hand to his face to shield himself from the bright sun that crested over the distant hills. His other hand went for his side arm.

"Easy there, Ryder," Turk said.

Sean blinked away the sleep and adjusted his head so that Turk's body stood between himself and the sun. Sean propped himself up on his elbows and looked around the camp. He and Turk were the only ones who appeared to be awake.

"Time is it?" Sean asked.

"After six," Turk replied.

Sean shook his head. He'd lain down at two a.m. Jules should have woken him at four, but apparently his partner hadn't managed to remain awake through his shift, leaving them vulnerable for at least the last two hours.

"Come on," Turk said. "Me and you need to take a walk."

Sean picked himself up off the ground and stretched out the kinks. He followed Turk away from the camp, casting a look down at his partner, who was sleeping while leaning back against their packs. During Sean's shift, the night had been silent. No howls. No movement. Nothing at all, in fact, and that concerned him. It made him wary that whatever those *things* were, they were close by, and every living creature made sure to get as far away from them as possible. He couldn't help but think that's what they should do, as well.

He caught up to Turk and said, "Why isn't anybody else up?"

"Some are," Turk said without looking back. "They're waiting. Conserving energy."

Sean thought about asking what for, but didn't. Instead, he said, "Where're we going? Back to last night's location?"

Turk turned his head a notch or two, and looked at Sean out of the corner of his eye. "Nothing to see there." Then he picked up his pace and pulled a few feet ahead. Was that a hint that Sean should shut his mouth?

Sean kept a few feet of distance between himself and Turk as they ascended a dirt-packed hill that rose two hundred feet or so into the air. Sean kept looking back over his shoulder every thirty seconds to get a wider view of the terrain below them. He located the path he and Jules had taken to reach the SEAL team the night before. He wasn't sure, but he thought he might have seen the spot where the attack occurred. Thick vegetation walled both sides of the area. It made sense that those *things* would hide in there. Not that anything about them made sense to Sean.

Turk stopped a few feet shy of the smooth hill crest and turned to face Sean. He said, "All right, here's the deal."

Sean crossed the distance between them and stopped. He faced Turk and mirrored his stance and said nothing.

"Delta Force came through here a week ago. They communicated that they had run into forces of," he paused and wiped the sweat from his brow, leaving a discernible line across the bottom of his forehead like a squeegee on a windshield, "humanoid beings. Apparently, that's the exact phrase they used. They located an underground facility, scouted it. They saw no one enter or exit, but continued to run into these, *things*. One or two at a time. They lost nobody on their team, and managed to take out everyone they encountered." He stopped and gave Sean a slight nod, as if asking if he were following along.

"Okay," Sean said. "Guess that means I'm not crazy."

"No," Turk said. "I thought so last night, though. I received this information less than an hour ago."

"So why are you telling me and not your guys?"

"I'm getting to that."

"Okay."

"Can I continue?"

Sean extended his hand. "Go ahead."

"They lay in wait for about four days, again, Delta, watching. They see a truck pull up to the entrance and block it. A couple guys get out. They look like they are armed to the teeth and wearing body armor. At least, that's the impression the Delta guys relayed after viewing the men for a couple seconds. They disappear behind the truck, then the truck drives off and the men are no longer in sight. Gone inside, supposedly. The order comes from above that Delta is to infiltrate the place."

"Why?" Sean asked.

Turk shrugged, brought his hand up and scratched the stubble along his jawline. "I wasn't given that information. I was told that Delta had to wait for the Rangers to arrive. They were being sent in to provide backup and security."

Sean felt a lump rise in his throat. "Battalion?"

"Third," Turk said.

"Company?"

"Bravo."

Sean exhaled. He knew that they wouldn't be in Nigeria right now if members of Delta Force and Bravo Company of the Third Battalion of the U.S. Army Rangers didn't need to be rescued or recovered.

He felt relieved, too.

Sean's brother, Nick, was a Ranger.

Third Battalion.

Alpha Company.

"Don't worry," Turk said. "If it was your brother's Company, you wouldn't be here."

Sean lifted a curious eyebrow. He was not aware that Turk knew about his brother. "Okay, so what's the deal then? Some of them were killed? Guys hurt? Taken? Are we in rescue or recovery mode?"

Turk shrugged and shook his head as he lowered his eyes toward the ground. "We don't know, Ryder. Delta went in, and the Rangers didn't hear anything. They went in, and no one has heard from any of them since. It's been ninety-six hours of total silence."

Sean felt a cold bead of sweat drip down his back and settle into the waistband of his pants. Shivers branched out along its path, tracing his nerves. He grabbed his canteen, took a sip of water. "Why are you telling me this?"

Turk looked up and made eye contact with Sean. "Well, you and Jules are here because of potential trauma to the victims, maybe even to my team. I brought you up here because you encountered one of those *things*. We all heard them, as much as we don't want to admit it. But you saw one. Jules did, too, but he seems worthless now. What on earth could scare a man like him that much? How did that thing move? How did it react? Eleven shots, man. Did all of them hit?"

Sean nodded. "Every bullet hit. The first three dead center. He... it stumbled for a second, but kept moving. Hell, he moved faster than I've ever seen a man move, and that was after I shot him."

Turk massaged his temples and nodded, presumably taking in the information.

"It wasn't until Jules got a head shot that it, the guy, went down," Sean said. "Look, Turk, I saw the body both alive and dead. I can tell you one thing for certain. It might have looked human, but it had no soul."

Turk turned away, leaned his head back. It looked like he was surveying the short distance from where the two men stood to the top of the hill.

Sean followed the man's gaze and made his own assessment of the area. He knew if there was a secret underground facility, they'd have monitoring or security devices spread across the area. Or were those beings the only security the facility needed? Then a thought crossed Sean's mind that scared him to his core. What if the underground facility was full of an army of those *things*? What if they bred or created them there?

He saw the look on Turk's face and felt certain that the SEAL team leader had the same thoughts.

"Okay," Turk said. "Nice and easy to the top. The entrance is in the ground, past the hill. I want to scout the area and get everyone ready to move."

"You going to tell them what you told me?" Sean asked.

Turk shook his head. "Just the basics. I don't know if they could handle the rest. Shit, I don't know if I can handle it." He took a deep breath, blew the air out in a long stream. "I'm going to tell them about Delta and the Rangers and that we think some are dead and some are being held hostage. We're going to operate on the presumption that this is a rescue mission, but I'll prepare them that they need to be ready for a battle."

Sean nodded and said nothing in reply.

"Okay," Turk said. "Let's get to the top."

Both men crouched as they neared the crest of the hill, dropped to their knees, flattened onto their stomachs. Sean pulled out a scope and surveyed the land beyond the hill. He scanned inch by inch, looking for anything out of the ordinary. He tried to find signs of survivors or the bodies of the dead. However, all he saw was scorched brown earth and thick inhospitable shrubs.

"I got it," Turk said as he extended a muscular arm and pointed with his index finger. "Over there."

Sean moved the scope to the side and followed an imaginary line extending from Turk's finger. He saw a spot on the ground where the dirt didn't match its surroundings. It was loose and browner that the rest, like it had been turned over recently.

"See it?" Turk asked.

"Yeah," Sean replied. "I see it." He brought the scope to his eye and studied the area surrounding the hidden entrance. Nothing seemed out of place. If there were any security measures taken, he couldn't spot them from the top of the hill. He knew they'd have to be careful when they approached. Setting off an IED would not only be deadly for the team, it would also alert whoever was below ground to their presence.

"We're gonna wait here for a little bit," Turk said. "I want to see if anyone, or anything, comes or goes."

"Okay," Sean said against his better judgment. He didn't want to stay there, on top of the hill. What if those *things* were watching them from behind? He didn't think he was in a position to argue with Turk over how they should handle the mission, though. He remained flat on his stomach, studying every square foot of land between himself and the hidden entrance to the underground facility. He scanned the area to the left and to the right, a hundred feet in either direction. Sean wanted to make sure that he could navigate the area with his eyes closed if necessary.

"It's opening," Turk said.

The words took a moment to filter through Sean's brain. He'd been studying a spot where the dirt appeared to be disturbed. The mound of soil was much too large to be the location of an IED, though. It appeared to be about six feet long and two feet wide. A grave, he presumed. There were a couple dozen of them scattered throughout that section of the landscape.

"Ryder," Turk said. "Look."

Sean let his eyes float back to their natural position and then inched his head to the right until his gaze settled on the dirt-covered entrance, which was now propped open a few feet. A pale hand reached out and wrapped around the edge of the door. A matching hand poked out and flattened onto the dirt. Sean moved his scope into position to get a better look. Matted and tangled brown hair appeared next, semi-parted in the middle and hanging over the face of the person exiting the facility. A female form emerged, clothed only in a tattered gown that had probably been white at one time, but now was stained dark red and brown. Sean didn't want to acknowledge the possible causes of the stains.

"Sweet fuzzy ducks, what are we looking at?" Turk said.

Sean squinted, as if the action might provide him with a better view. The woman started walking in their direction. She shook her head side to side, the motion jerky, then she reached up and pulled her hair out of her face, tucking it behind her ears. Sean gasped at the sight of her face. Her eyes were bright and golden brown. Her skin was pale, with dark purple rings surrounding her lips and eyes. She had a gash on her left cheek that gaped open an inch. Faint traces of dark red smeared the area between the cut and her chin, but the wound had stopped bleeding some time ago. The edges of her severed skin were black, appeared to be infected.

"What in God's name are we looking at?" Turk said.

"I don't know," Sean said. "Like I said, they aren't human."

The woman kept shuffling in their direction, stopped. Her eyes closed, revealing purple eyelids. Her head dropped back. She rotated her head to the left, then the right. Her nostrils flared open. She appeared to be trying to sense if something, or someone, was nearby.

"What is—"

Sean jabbed his hand into Turk's side and let out a quick shushing sound. He didn't say anything. If that female thing heard them and started toward them, they'd be forced to kill it. Sean wanted to see what she would do, hoping it would give them an idea how to detect and possibly avoid unnecessary encounters.

The woman's head returned to its natural position, and she opened her eyes. They seemed even brighter, and without looking back, Sean figured that a cloud had slid past the sun, letting its rays hit the woman in her face. She turned to her right and shuffled toward the mounds of dirt Sean had noticed earlier.

"I thought you said they were fast," Turk whispered.

"They are," Sean said. "I guess only when they want to be, or need to be."

"Come on. Let's get back to camp and get everyone ready to move."

Sean continued to follow the woman with his scope. "Wait. I want to see what she does."

"What?" Turk said.

"Serious. This might help us later."

"Five more minutes. Got it?"

Sean nodded and then returned to watching the woman. At the first grave she came to, she bent over and grabbed a fistful of dirt. Her hand lifted the dirt from the ground to her face. She brought her other hand up and held the loosened earth in both hands. Tiny rivers of brown fell from the cracks between her fingers and cascaded to the ground. She placed her nose in the center of her palms. Sean heard her moans carried on the wind, and then the woman let her hands slip apart and watched the dirt as it fell back on top of the grave. She repeated the process again at a second grave, then moved on to a third. This time, when she brought the dirt to her face and stuck her nose in it, her body straightened and became rigid. Her arms lifted and the soil fell from her hands. Some of it was swept away with the wind, while the remainder of it fell across her hair and shoulders. Then the woman let out a piercing scream before falling to her knees and letting her torso cover the mound that Sean presumed held the body of someone she loved.

Chapter 5

The team moved out as the final rays of the sun were swallowed up behind the horizon, casting long shadows across the camp. Anything the men didn't carry with them had been buried two feet in the ground. The packed soil hadn't been easy to dig up, but Turk had said he felt better if all traces of them being there were removed. Sean didn't have anything left over, but he pitched in and helped the other men who did.

Turk had given the team a watered down version of the events. He had said that they were there to rescue members of Delta Force and Bravo Company of the U.S. Army Rangers Third Battalion. He didn't give his men false hope that they'd find all of the men alive, though the mission was still classified as rescue and not recovery. He warned all of them to be prepared to face extreme danger once they breeched the entrance of the facility.

Turk appeared to deviate from the tactics that Sean expected. He kept all the men close. They didn't question him, although the looks in their eyes appeared to cast doubt on how he was leading them. Sean wondered if he was reading them wrong because he knew something they didn't.

Jules and Sean stayed toward the back of the group as they climbed the hill. Every few seconds, Sean found himself looking over his shoulders to see if something was following them. He no longer believed he'd see a person following the group. Those beings were not human. Not anymore, at least.

They stopped at the top of the hill and everyone dropped to the ground. Each SEAL had an assignment at that point, and they carried out their duties.

Sean immediately turned his attention to the graveyard. He wondered how long the woman had stayed out there. Had she had truly been grieving, or were her actions some primal instinct that was carried out because of a series of electrical pulses from the deepest recesses of her brain?

"Shit," Turk said from Sean's right.

Sean adjusted his head and looked toward the hidden entrance to the facility and saw two armed men crouching near it. They appeared to be human, although Sean wasn't sure he could be positive about that.

Turk whistled and Ruiz and Gilmore crawled forward. They each set up their RAD M91A2 sniper rifles and settled themselves in preparation of the shot.

One shot, one kill, thought Sean. Though technically the slogan of Marine Scout Snipers, he found it to be appropriate for the current situation. He watched the men who guarded the dirt covered entrance. The only parts of their bodies that moved were their eyes. Sean wondered if perhaps the men had taken notice of the group and had sent a silent alert into the facility, preparing another dozen or so armed guards in anticipation of the team's next move.

Turk gave the signal to Ruiz and Gilmore, and the two men fired in unison, each sending a single .300 Winchester Magnum .30 caliber bullet toward the heads of the unsuspecting men that guarded the entrance.

Sean held his breath as he watched the heads of the men flinch upon impact. A dark hole in each man's forehead signaled the entry wound. Blood trickled, then flowed freely. Although he couldn't see the exit wounds, he assumed the bullets did their job and destroyed most of the gray matter inside their heads, as well as the backs of their skulls. He knew if he were closer and had the proper lighting, he'd see a pink cloud consisting mostly of blood, but also brain and skull, falling to the ground.

All fourteen men waited in silence. Sean presumed that Turk wanted to wait and see if the guards were being monitored by forces inside the facility. If so, they'd come out through the entrance, the perfect bottleneck, within the next minute or two. Or perhaps they'd unleash some other kind of attack. Sean didn't want to think about that, though. He continued with the belief that if someone was going to come and retaliate, they'd be human and a single bullet to the chest would stop them.

The final twinges of pinkish-red sky faded behind the horizon. Sean switched to his night vision goggles. He tried to remain focused on the entrance, but his sights kept drifting toward the graveyard. Perhaps it was simply human nature, a need to fill in the blanks and have all questions answered, but he couldn't stop wondering what was buried under the dirt mounds. Had those *things* buried the man Jules had killed the night before, perhaps alongside the bodies of the creatures Delta had killed? Or were the bodies that lay there those of humans who perished at the hands of the beings?

Sean saw the outline of a hunched-over figure moving at a slow pace between two rows of loose dirt. Even from this distance, the eyes stood out against the rest of the body. Sean was sure that if he could see the thing up close and without night vision goggles on, those eyes would glow brown or green or blue, even in the dark. The figure stopped next to one of the gravesites. Sean waited to see if it would lean over, presumably to scoop up dirt and sniff it, possibly in an attempt to find a loved one. But the being didn't bend, nor did it reach into the dirt. Instead, it straightened and dropped its head back. He remembered how the woman had done the same thing earlier that day, her eyes closed and nostrils flared wide. At that moment, he also became aware of a light wind blowing against the back of his sweaty neck. The breeze that cooled him would also carry their scent in the direction of the graveyard, and that thing.

Sean scooted back until he was below the ridgeline. "Turk," he whispered.

Turk looked over his shoulder, crawled backward until he was next to Sean.

"What?" Turk said.

Sean took a breath and then said, "There's one in the graveyard. I think it knows we're here."

"Why?"

"It changed posture, like the woman, or thing, earlier today. I get the feeling they do that to, I don't know, maybe sense what's around."

Turk nodded, said nothing.

"And the wind is blowing in that direction. It's carrying our scent right to it."

Turk reached up and rubbed his eyes, leaving smudges of dirt on his cheeks. "Okay." He shifted into a crouching position and approached Gilmore. "Gilly," he said. "Scan the area to your left. It might look like a graveyard, mounds of dirt on the ground and shit. You see anything alive in there, shoot it."

Gilmore nodded, adjusted his rifle and his position so he could scout the graveyard.

"Make it a head shot," Turk added.

Sean resumed his position at the top of the hill and relocated the being. It was moving, shuffling in their direction. Its right foot would step forward, then its left would drag along the ground, foot cockeyed, until both legs were even. Sean wondered if the man they encountered the night before moved this way when walking. Perhaps these *things* walked slowly when they didn't have a purpose. Only when their intent was to hurt or kill, or maybe even feed, did they move fast.

The thing stopped again, now about halfway between the men and the graveyard. The distance was deceiving, though. The last third would be uphill, and with as slow as it walked, that would take a while. Even if it sprinted toward their position, the uphill climb was certain to slow it down.

"Gilly, what's taking so long?" Turk said, a little too loud, mirroring Sean's thoughts exactly.

"Frickin' trying to line up this shot," Gilmore said. "His head... the damn thing moves in my scope."

"What do you mean it moves?" Turk said. "I'm watching it. It's still as a damn rock."

"Moves isn't the right word," Gilmore said. "It shimmers."

Turk cursed and rose up a foot or two to pass over the four men between him and Gilmore. He dropped to his stomach, and Sean felt a puff of wind and a thin layer of dirt coat his face.

"Let me see your rifle," Turk said.

Gilmore shifted to his right and Turk maneuvered himself behind the weapon. He placed his eye to the scope. "Where the frig is it?"

A sliver of panic passed through Sean. He swung his head to the left and scanned the area below them. The thing had disappeared.

"I don't see it," Sean said.

At that moment, a shrill shriek erupted from no more than twenty feet from them. As soon as the sound had passed, the thing hovered over Gilmore and flipped him over and then swiped at the SEAL's neck. Gilmore's screams were drowned in the blood that spewed forth from the gaping hole in his throat.

Turk was the first to react. He rose to his knees and swung the M91A2 around. Three bullets remained in the magazine. He fired all three in rapid succession. The first hit the thing in the abdomen, only causing a slight reaction in the form of a grunt. The next two shots were perfect, one smashing into the center of its forehead, and the other on the right side, an inch above the ear.

Sean watched as its body folded over and fell to the ground in a heap, still and silent.

"Ryder, Jules," Turk said, slowly and deeply. "Help Gilly."

Sean remained frozen for a minute as he processed what had happened. He had to compartmentalize it and focus on helping Gilmore. That's what he and Jules were there for. The SEALs had medical training, but PJs were the most prepared to deal with combat injuries, especially life-threatening wounds. He grabbed Jules by the collar and both men rushed to Gilmore's body, each taking a side. They pulled him down the hillside a few feet so that the tops of their heads weren't exposed over the hill crest.

"Need light," Sean said.

Someone shone a light over his shoulder, aiming the strong beam at Gilmore's head. The light reflected off of the man's dull and lifeless eyes. The grievous wound had severed both carotid arteries, and what little blood pressure remained pumped out what was left of his blood. Sean knew at that moment there was no point in attempting resuscitation, but he and Jules did everything they could. Kneeling in a pool of a mixture of Gilmore's and the being's blood, Sean applied pressure to the dead man's neck.

The team was quiet. There were no words of encouragement. Every man could tell Gilmore was gone by the amount of blood on the ground and the size of the hole in his neck.

"Stop," Turk said.

Sean rocked back on his heels and looked down at his soaked crimson-colored hands. He felt drops of fluid falling from his fingers and splattering on his pants.

The sounds of nature had disappeared. There were no chirping birds. The ever-present hum of insects could no longer be heard.

The men looked at one another then crept up to the hilltop.

Sean saw the outlines of five or six beings at the foot of the hill. The quiet night was soon full of their howls and shrieks as they ascended the hill toward the team. Or perhaps toward the body in an attempt to recover it. A hail of gunfire erupted around Sean. He noticed Jules collapse onto his back and worried for a second that his partner had been hit, or attacked by one of those *things*. Jules reached down and grabbed his pistol from his thigh holster, then rolled over and began firing. Sean did the same.

After a minute of incessant gunfire, the air smelled of cordite and the area was still and quiet again, save for the high-pitched hum in Sean's ears. He scanned the area below them and saw bodies scattered across the hillside. None of the bodies moved, and none appeared to be breathing. Instinctively, he looked toward the graveyard to see if any more were approaching. His gut told him that's where the ones they'd gunned down came from, even if he only recalled seeing one. Relief flooded his system when he saw that the area between them and the graveyard and the entrance to the facility was empty. He wasn't sure if it was misplaced or not, but at that moment he felt that they'd be safer inside.

Turk started down the hill, and without a word spoken, his team followed. Everyone moved with a sense of urgency, masking the pain they all felt at the loss of Gilmore.

"We better go," Sean said to Jules, who nodded in response.

They descended the hill, wasting no time crossing the remaining distance to the entrance. Turk headed to the right and inspected the body of one of the deceased guards. He shone a light over the man and dug through his pockets, producing a bundle that appeared to hold an ID card.

"Christ," Turk said. "I don't think these were guards."

"Why's that?" Sean said.

"This badge indicates he's part of a NATO force." Turk looked back at his men. "Someone check the other guy."

Bates returned a moment later with an ID card and said, "Same with this guy."

"What were they doing then?" Sean said.

Turk shook his head. "I don't know. Maybe these are fake? To get them in and out of the area?"

"Maybe you should call it in?" Sean said.

"Nah," Turk said. "Not right now. Let's get inside."

Two men worked on the entrance door while the rest took position and watched over the area. At this point, they knew they had to be ready for an attack originating from anywhere. The beings were capable of getting there in the blink of an eye, so they had to be spotted and dealt with at once.

Turk and Sean slipped through the opening first. They hunched and squatted down in an effort to move through a tunnel that angled downward. The faint glow of light could be seen, and it looked like the tunnel curved before it reached the source of the illumination. It took the two men about a minute to reach the other end of the shaft.

Despite everything that had happened in the previous twenty-four hours, Sean found himself unprepared for what he saw as he crouched down and stuck his legs out of the tunnel, lowering them to the floor. He ducked his head, clearing the overhang, and then straightened his body. Fluorescent light fixtures cast a dim yellow glow over the area. There were trails of blood on the ground. The fluid was of varying shades of red and different textures, indicating how fresh or old it was. Some spots were considerably darker than others, and Sean realized those spots didn't contain blood, but rather human feces scraped along the ground as if dragged by feet that didn't, or perhaps couldn't, break contact with the floor. Bloody handprints lined the walls from floor to ceiling. In some spots, thick rivers of crimson flowed from the prints on the wall to the floor. There were deep scratches etched into the wall and he found himself imagining some deranged being clawing at the walls with bloody stumps where fingernails had once been.

"What the holy hell happened here?" Turk said from behind Sean.

Sean shook his head. He found no words to describe what he felt. His eyes continued to scan the hallway. He saw offices with busted windows. Lights flickered throughout the hall and in the rooms.

Finally, the entire team filled the small area of the lobby. Everyone remained silent and stood in place, presumably contemplating what had happened to create the macabre scene they stood before. The place was quiet. Good, in a way, because it helped Sean feel that danger was not imminent. On the other hand, he had the distinct feeling that something was watching them, and if the team didn't make the correct move, it would pounce without warning.

"All right," Turk said as he pushed to the front of the group. "We need to find a secure location for command. Let's get moving."

Chapter 6

The sound of the group moving the through the hall echoed inside Sean's head. He knew he heard it because his training had attuned him to listening for such things. Reality was that they moved down the hall as a silent amoeba, shifting as the group changed shape when necessary. Sean and Jules were in the middle of the group, shielded by SEALs on all sides.

The buzz from the light fixtures above them rose and fell as they passed underneath them. Every so often, a light appeared to be on the fritz, flickering between low and high illumination like a strobe light, or cutting off entirely.

They came to a corner office set against an intersecting hallway. Sean craned his head to check the darkened corridor. To his left, the hall dead ended after ten feet. To the right, it extended further than he could see because of the darkness. The lights had either burned out, or been smashed out. He didn't think either option was out of the realm of possibility.

He slipped between the men next to him and stepped into the open doorway of the empty office. The windows surrounding the room on both sides had been broken. Jagged shards of glass remained attached to the frame, while tinier fragments littered the floor. The wooden door was split down the middle, and only attached to one set of hinges. If Sean touched it, he was sure it would sway like a pendulum, scraping along the floor. A monitor lay face down on the desk. He saw a keyboard upside down on the floor, several of its keys scattered throughout the office. He noticed a small puddle of blood on the corner of the desk and the floor below it. Upon further inspection, he saw a clump of hair and bloodied scalp attached to the sharp corner.

It was the fifth office they had passed, but Turk hadn't shown any intention of stopping to investigate. Why? Did he know more than he had let on? He had given Sean plenty of information, but there were pieces of the story missing. Things that didn't make sense, perhaps because they couldn't make sense.

Sean left the office and quickly and silently resumed his position within the group. The man next to him shook his head and shot him a look. But Sean didn't care. They were in unfamiliar territory, and he justified his actions as being potentially helpful later on if he found himself roaming these halls while struggling to survive. There was no field manual for what they had seen, or for what he feared they would encounter in the pits of the facility.

Turk lifted a fist into the air and stopped. He hunched over and moved to his left, then stuck his head inside an office through a hole in a smashed window. He pulled out of the hole and made eye contact with Sean.

"Come on," he said.

Sean pushed past the men next to him again and met Turk near the office door. Turk had his hand on the knob and began turning it.

"What is it?" Sean said.

Turk shook his head, then leaned his shoulder into the door and pushed it open. They were greeted with the foul smell of a decomposing body. In the hall, the smell of the corpse had mixed with blood and feces and ammonia, and had gone unnoticed. Except, it seemed, by Turk. However, inside the office, the stench was enough to cause Sean's stomach to turn.

"Where's the body?" Sean said, looking over Turk's shoulders in an attempt to get a better look around.

Turk reached out and spun an office chair. The black leather chair swung to the right and came to a stop dead center in front of the two men. A faceless figure slumped in the seat. Its hands were missing. So were its legs below the knees. Dark blood caked the jagged ends where extremities had once protruded.

"What the frig?" Sean said as he backed up until he hit the wall.

Turk took a step forward, leaned over, placed his hands on his knees, appeared to be investigating the remains of the man's face. Turk's head dropped to the left, then the right, then he straightened his body and turned at the waist, making eye contact with Sean.

"Bite marks," Turk said.

"What?" Sean said.

"Someone chewed his face off."

Sean steeled himself and took four steps forward. He stopped next to Turk and leaned over, placing his left hand on his knee and keeping the other on his Beretta M9 semiautomatic 9mm pistol. He held his breath as he placed his face closer to the remains of whoever had once occupied the seat. The nose was missing, and so were the eyes. All that was left were hollow sockets that had been gouged bare. The flesh around the cheeks had been stripped off in chunks, down to the bone in some spots. It looked like Turk had been correct in his assumption. The edges of the wounds showed the distinct patterns of bite marks. Sean glanced down at the stubby arms and legs and wondered if whoever, or whatever, had done this to the man's face, had also chewed off his extremities.

Sean stood and took a couple steps back. His head felt heavy, drowning under the weight of the discovery. Was this all a dream? Surely, there was no possible way they could have seen any of what they'd seen over the last twenty-four hours.

Gunfire erupted in the distance, and Sean, with his hand still on the handle of his M9, retrieved his pistol and spun toward the sound of the shots.

Turk pushed past Sean and exited the office, resuming his spot at the head of the group. The SEAL team dropped into position, each man covering another and watching an area of the hall. Two men took off toward the sound of the gunfire without being told. They stopped further down the hall, at the edge of the intersection with the dark corridor.

The spattering of bullets, and the echo they produced throughout the hall, ended almost as abruptly as they began.

For the first time that day, Sean felt that their mission might include rescue, and not only recovery. He considered the possibility that one of those *things* had a weapon, but dismissed the thought. His experience so far, as limited as it was, indicated that the beings didn't have the instincts to use weapons. They didn't need them, judging by how easily one had killed Gilmore.

"All right, everybody," Turk said. "We're gonna investigate down there, but not until we've reached the end of the perimeter hallway."

Sean fell back in formation and the group began moving again. He felt as though he moved with a purpose now that there was a possibility of finding someone alive. It didn't matter who it was. He hoped they could get there in time to save them. He looked to his right to share his enthusiasm with Jules, and saw the man struggling to keep his eyes open.

"You doing all right?" Sean said.

Jules turned his head and nodded. "Yeah. A bit tired and my head hurts. But I'll be OK."

Jules was sweating profusely, but under the circumstances, Sean didn't put too much weight into that. The air in the facility was stagnant. He assumed that the underground building's ventilation system had ceased to operate. He didn't bother to presume as to why, though.

One by one, in rapid succession, the lights in the hall blinked out starting from the far end of the corridor. The buzzing sound they created diminished until it disappeared altogether.

"Dammit," Turk said.

A few seconds later, dull red emergency lights turned on. They were anchored to the wall near the ceiling and surrounded by thick metal cages. Sean wondered if the facility had lost power and the generator was slow to kick on. Or, worse, it had already been running on generator power and the fuel had run out.

"Extra caution," Turk said. "Careful if you have to shoot. Make damn sure it's not one of us you got your sights on."

One man chuckled, but the rest remained quiet. The atmosphere was somber, and with good reason.

A series of howls and shrieks and yells erupted throughout the building. They came at the group from both directions, echoing and bouncing off the walls and the floors and the ceiling. Sean lifted his hands to his ears and twisted at the waist, expecting to see an army of the creatures coming at them from the front and from behind. But there was nothing. Then the calls that roared through the corridor faded to silence. Perhaps the noise was their reaction to the lights going out. Or maybe it was something else.

Celebration?

Maybe the last survivor, the man wielding the gun, had succumbed to the beings.

"Let's go," Turk said from the front of the group.

They continued down the hall, passing office after office. All had been ransacked, not a one of them spared. Sean noticed another body sprawled across a desk, and soon this became the norm, rather than the exception. They weren't the soldiers the men were looking for, though. If Sean had to place them, he'd figure them to be people who had worked in the facility.

The red emergency lights cut off, and after a second or two, the fluorescent hall lights turned back on, although Sean thought they seemed dimmer than before. With the hall illuminated again, he noticed that the corridor came to an end about a hundred feet ahead. It appeared that another lit hallway connected to it. The group slowed down as they approached the end. Turk signaled to Bellows and Steele, and the two men moved ahead of the group. They pressed against the interior wall and made their way to the corner.

Steele led the way. When he reached the corner, he dropped to a knee and Bellows pushed up tight to him. They both peered around the corner together, allowing the barrels of their HK MP7 submachine guns to precede them.

Steele signaled to the group, and Turk began moving. The rest of the men followed without hesitation.

Sean rounded the corner and saw that the walls that lined the hallway were solid. No windows or doors as far as he could see. He figured the outer wall, to his left, butted up to solid rock, or at least packed earth. There appeared to be a recessed section on the interior wall a couple hundred feet ahead on the right. Another hallway, he figured, one that might cut through the center of the facility.

Ten bodies were scattered throughout the hall. They lay on the floor, motionless and with obvious catastrophic injuries.

What was worse was that they were all clothed in ACUs, Army Combat Uniforms.

Sean swallowed hard in an attempt to force the lump in his throat down. He knew that the bodies they saw were those of the Rangers who'd been sent in to provide security and backup for Delta.

"Check each one," Turk said. "But don't linger. From where I'm standing, they don't look alive."

Sean noted the grotesque wounds on their bodies. Some had been killed, leaving the men to look like they were sleeping, except for the mortal wounds to their heads, necks or chests. Others had been mutilated in such a way that he felt like it ruled out a human being responsible for the death. There was no way one man could do that to another.

He and Jules assessed each man as two teams of three SEALs watched over them. The process was quick, and it didn't require more than a glance to pronounce each man dead. All of them, even the ones that weren't mutilated, showed signs of decomposition, leading Sean to believe the deaths occurred more than forty-eight hours ago.

Sean looked up after pronouncing the last body and saw that Turk and the other SEALs had moved ahead and were walking along the exterior wall. They stopped at a spot where he assumed Turk had a view of the open area Sean had noticed when they first started their trek down this section of the facility.

Turk looked back at Sean and the others and signaled for them to approach. The group moved together along the interior wall and came to a stop fifteen feet from Turk.

Turk crossed the hall and said, "I think we've found our command room."

Sean moved closer and saw a twenty-foot expanse of window still intact. It appeared as though it had been impacted, perhaps by bullets, but the glass had not shattered. Bloody handprints were scattered along the glass, but they had not made a dent in it. They wouldn't, Sean figured, just like bullets wouldn't. The glass was impenetrable.

Behind the windows were banks of computers and monitors, some on and others off. There was a single door leading in, and another one against the far wall, but the second door was solid steel, so there was no way to tell what was behind it. It could've been a closet or a door to another office.

Collins and Brady were the first to approach the room. They found the door to be locked. However, with the aid of a specialized set of tools, they managed to open it and take control of their new command room.

Chapter 7

The SEAL team investigated every nook and cranny of the room. Karl and Metz moved from computer to computer performing a quick check to determine whether or not the machines held information that would have been deemed critical.

Sean and Jules hung back against the rear wall, watching the men work. Judging by the looks on the men's faces, Sean figured they'd all be happy to wait it out in the bulletproof room until additional forces arrived. He knew none of them would admit it, though. Still, he couldn't blame them if they felt that way. It was the way he felt after seeing the condition of the bodies they'd passed in the hall, not to mention the things they had experienced outside.

"I'm never coming back to Nigeria, Jules," Sean said.

Jules nodded and said, "Man, me neither, and this is probably where my ancestors come from."

A quick laugh escaped Sean's mouth, drawing a curious look or two from the SEALs.

"Guess we shouldn't do that again," Sean said.

"What's this *we* stuff?" Jules said. "You're the one losing control in here."

Sean felt like laughing again. It wasn't that he found anything particularly amusing. He figured it was his mind's way of coping with the situation. How many men, U.S. soldiers and highly trained ones at that, had entered this facility? Fifty? More? How many had exited?

None. A big fat friggin' zero.

In Sean's mind, that meant his chances of ever stepping foot on solid earth again, as well as the chances of Jules and the entire SEAL team doing the same, were slim to none.

Sean noticed that the SEALs were standing around, all except for Karl and Metz who still had four computers to check. Turk stood directly across from Sean, the SEAL team leader's eyes locked on his. Turk held his MK 14 EBR in both hands, across his abdomen, aimed at nothing. An HK MP7 was strapped across Turk's chest, and Sean knew from working with the man that Turk could change weapons faster than most men could unzip their pants.

For two minutes, the men stared at each other. Neither looked away. Neither man blinked. The look in Turk's eyes and on his face was one that Sean was familiar with. It was the look of a brave man who knew that death was certain. He'd seen it in every man he'd been unable to save. That point when a mission went from rescue to recovery. They stared at death and refused to let the reaper believe he had any power over them. The only question Sean had was whether or not that was the look on his own face.

The room was quiet except for the faint hum of the lights, the weak *whirr* of a fan—something that Sean had not noticed in the building until now—and the sounds of Karl and Metz banging on keyboards. Metz stopped and stood and moved toward the final computer. All eyes focused on the man. He took a seat and grabbed a mouse and placed his hands over the keyboard. A minute later, Karl dragged a seat across the aisle. Squeaky wheels in desperate need of oiling broke the silence. Karl picked up the chair and carried it the final three feet, then placed it on the ground and sat next to Metz.

The two men spoke to one another in hushed tones, too low for Sean to figure out what they were saying. Geek speak, Sean figured. He wouldn't have understood it anyway.

The lights dimmed and flickered. Metz cursed out loud, perhaps worried that he was going to lose power to the computer. And if he was worried about that, it probably meant that he had found something.

Sean pushed off the wall and took a few steps forward. Apparently, Turk had the same thought, because he started moving toward Metz at the same time.

"Turk," Metz said. "I got something we can use."

"What is it?" Turk said as he picked his way through the men. He came to a stop three feet from the team's resident IT specialists and narrowed his eyes as he looked down at the screen. "That what I think it is?"

"Blueprints," Metz said. "The entire facility. Look," he pointed toward the screen, "we're on the first floor. That locked door in the back of the room leads below, but whatever's down there doesn't connect to anything else on the floor below us."

"So this corridor wraps around on all four sides," Turk said, "but stops halfway in the front and doesn't connect with the hall we came in through."

"That's right," Metz said.

"Stairs at the end of the dark hallway we passed," Turk said. "The one we heard gunfire from." He glanced around the room. The rest of the team nodded in agreement with his statement.

"Yeah," Metz said. "And the hall parallel, the one this connects to, has an adjoining half hallway that leads to another set of stairs down. It cuts through the middle of the facility, like the dark hall where we heard the gunshots coming from. They don't meet though."

Sean moved closer to where Turk stood and began making a mental diagram in case he found himself separated from Turk and had to find his way through the building.

"Where's the diagrams for the next floor?" Turk asked.

Metz adjusted the mouse and scrolled. "There."

"All right," Turk said. "It looks like the floor we're on is halls and offices or whatever, but packed earth in the middle. But the floor below this one, there's no gaps. Look, four big rooms in the corners with a wide hall, maybe, between them. Then it looks like the center of the floor is walled, but there's open space and some smaller rooms."

"And there's a third floor," Karl said. "Mirrors the second."

Turk leaned forward and took control of the mouse. "Yeah, except the rooms in the corners are bigger. There's no smaller rooms on that floor. Halls and walls, and those big-ass rooms."

"What do you think they're for?" Sean asked.

Turk looked over his shoulder and stared at Sean for a moment before responding. "I hope that's where the men who came in here before us are being held."

"What if..." Sean stopped mid-sentence. He wanted to ask what if those *things* were being contained down there, but thought better of it.

"Yeah," Turk said. "No *what ifs* on this mission. We need to verify everything."

Sean glanced around the room and took note of the large blank screens hanging on the wall. "What about those?"

"I'd guess those screens were used for monitoring what's going on below," Karl said.

"Why aren't they on?" Turk asked.

"They're either run by one of these computers that's down," Karl replied, "or by another system that's down. This place seems to be working on little power. Why? Your guess is as good as mine."

"Fair enough," Turk said. "You think you can get them running?"

Karl shrugged. "I guess it's possible."

Turk moved to the middle of the room where he could face everyone. "Okay, then. Karl, you stay here with the PJs. The rest of us are—"

"Wait a minute," Sean said. "I'm not staying down here. I'm going with you."

"You're staying here," Turk said.

"What if someone out there needs medical assistance?"

"Then I'll make the determination how severe it is and if we think the guy has a chance, we'll bring him back here and you can provide the necessary medical assistance in here."

"This is bullshit," Sean said.

"What's bullshit is my guys having to watch your ass instead of their own."

Sean felt his face burn. Calling him, or any PJ for that matter, a liability was an insult. "We can handle ourselves, and for damn sure, *you* know that."

"Oh yeah?" Turk said. "You sure about that?" He pointed past Sean.

Sean turned his head and saw Jules leaning back against the wall, eyes closed, forehead covered in sweat.

"Counterpoint?" Turk said.

Sean shook his head. "Whatever. You win. We'll stay here."

Turk moved closer to Sean and placed his hand on Sean's shoulder. He leaned in close, spoke in a hushed tone. "It ain't about me winning and you losing. We're a team. This is now our command room and it's the safest place in the building. If something happens and only one of my guys survives, I need you safe and sound to make sure he gets out alive. This isn't a slight against you or PJs in general. Got it?"

Sean nodded and pulled away from Turk's grasp. "Yeah, I got it."

Turk lifted both hands in the air, but stopped short of placing his hands on Sean's shoulders again. "You and me are cool, Sean. You know that."

Sean said nothing. He looked past Turk and stared out the windows at the empty hallway. His eyes fixed on a dark stain that appeared to have been made when a bloodied head hit the wall and slid down it.

Turk backed up and made his way to the door that led to the corridor. "Let's go."

The SEAL team filed out of the room. Turk was the last to leave. He looked back at Sean and gave him a slight nod, as if to say *hold down the fort until I get back*. The door shut with a thump and a click, and Sean watched Turk walk beyond the bulletproof glass and then disappear from view.

The room was quiet again, except for the sounds of Karl tapping away at a keyboard.

Sean turned to Jules and slapped him across the face. His partner's skin felt cool and was covered in sweat.

Jules opened his eyes and furrowed his brow. "What?"

"I should be asking you that," Sean said. "What's wrong with you?"

Jules slouched back against the wall. "I don't know, man. Feel like I got the flu."

"Well, get your shit together. I got a feeling we're gonna be pretty busy soon." He hoped so, at least. His gut told him that the only thing they'd find in the building was dead bodies.

Jules nodded and said nothing.

Sean inhaled deeply, exhaled slowly. He studied his friend for a moment, then said, "Go sit down and get some rest. I'll get you up when we need you."

He didn't want to send Jules to take a nap, leaving himself as the only one who was watching the door, but he had to weigh the benefits of having Jules up now versus later. If the SEALs did succeed in rescuing survivors, it'd take both of them to assess their injuries and treat those most in need. Guys like Turk and Spencer could help. They had enough years in and had been through plenty of medical training. But Sean knew that there was no guarantee they'd be coming back.

"Uh, Sean," Jules said.

"Yeah?" Sean said.

"Look."

Sean lifted his eyes and looked at his friend. The man stood still, straight for the first time in twenty minutes. His eyes were wide and his mouth open an inch. Sean followed his gaze toward the front of the room. He retrieved his M9 and aimed it beyond the glass at the thing that shuffled down the hall.

"It's one of them," Jules said.

"I know," Sean said as he lowered his weapon, keeping both hands on it, and began moving toward the window. He'd already passed by Karl, but knew that the man was looking at the thing beyond the glass, because his fingers had stopped hammering away at the keyboard for the first time since Turk and the other SEALs had left the room.

"It's gonna get in here," Jules said.

"Shut up, Jules," Sean said. "Calm down."

"What in the world is that?" Karl said, now a step behind Sean.

Sean holstered his pistol as he stopped two feet from the window. He watched the woman on the other side of the window, at least it looked to be a woman, approach from his left. She wore a heavy coat, with a fur-lined hood. The hood sat atop her head and hung over her brow, shading her face. Three things gave her away to Sean as being not quite human. Her pale-white legs poked out from a tattered and dirty gown. Upon further inspection, Sean noted that the skin of her legs was lined with cuts, bruises, and streaks of dried blood. When she walked, she shuffled, managing to lift only her right foot a few inches off the ground. Her blue eyes seemed to glow in the shadows created by her hood.

He felt Karl pressed up against his right shoulder, and he turned to tell him to step back.

The man met his stare and said, "Do you see what I'm s—"

There was a loud bang on the glass and the muffled sound of a high-pitched scream followed. Sean stepped back and swung his head around. The woman, who'd been maybe ten feet away when he turned to look at Karl, now stood right in front of him. Her hood had fallen behind her head, and he saw that half her scalp had been pulled back. It hung down in a bloody sheet next to her neck, the weight of her blond hair pinning it down. Her arms were spread wide and she pounded on the glass repeatedly with the palms of her hands, leaving dirt and blood smudged on the window.

Karl pushed Sean to the side and pulled out his Sig Sauer P226 pistol. He fired two shots into the glass before Sean managed to knock the weapon out of the SEAL's hands.

"What're you gonna do with that, Karl?" Sean yelled.

"I... not sure..."

Sean shook his head and went to the window to inspect the damage. The bullet had hardly made a dent. He had been afraid that Karl's shots would weaken the integrity of the glass and any repeated banging by the woman would eventually cause the window to shatter. The glass held, though, and his fears subsided, for a moment at least.

The woman on the other side of the window had retreated against the far wall at the sound of the gunfire and bullets hitting the window. She was kneeling on the floor, her right arm covering her head. Sean found the behavior peculiar, and he wondered if these creatures were similar to humans in that they had their own quirks and fears and desires.

The woman rose from her crouched position and rushed the glass. Her appearance seemed distorted as she crossed the hall, almost like a blur. He recalled Gilmore saying that the man's head shimmered, up on the hill, moments before that same man killed him.

"She'll move on."

Sean spun around and planted his back against the glass. Karl did the same a few feet away from him. They both held their pistols out and aimed at the figure in the middle of the open doorway in the back of the room.

A small, fragile man with wisps of white hair atop his head and a thick white beard framing his face stepped out from the darkness. He held a pistol in his hand, but appeared to be careful not to aim it at the men.

Chapter 8

"What was that?" Turk cast a glance over his shoulder and saw that none of his men offered up an explanation in regards to the noise he'd heard. It sounded like a knock on a door, but so far the hallway walls were solid on both sides. No doors, no windows. A shriek followed the sound, but the sounds of people screaming had become commonplace, and he couldn't tell if the yell was related to the knocking. "All right, let's keep moving. Keep your eyes open."

The feeling that they were being followed had been with Turk the entire time they'd been inside the facility. It was something he couldn't shake, which was unusual. Turk was the kind of man who could push anything aside in order to focus on the task at hand.

He'd noticed the cameras when they exited the tunnel that led in from the outside. They were mounted near the ceiling throughout the facility and were protected by plastic bubbles. He figured the cameras were off, since they didn't move, and there weren't any indicator lights blinking. Then again, maybe whoever installed them was smart and placed electrical tape over the lights. It didn't matter, though. Turk was paranoid and he figured it was the presence of the cameras that made him so.

Or perhaps it was the fear that the building was full of those *things*.

The hallway opened up to the right, twenty feet ahead. They were near the center of the facility, close to the stairwell, still on the first floor. Turk stopped, motioned for Bates to step forward. He resumed walking once Bates fell in next to him. The two men moved on, took three steps, stopped to listen. Turk heard nothing other than the faint hum of the fluorescent lights. The sound had been present everywhere they'd been in the building, and it was a little unsettling that he hadn't tuned the noise out.

Turk and Bates stood five feet from the corner that led to the opening he expected would lead them to the stairwell. He stooped over and closed his eyes, hoping that doing so would enhance his other senses. It was a maneuver that had paid dividends in the past. Thirty seconds passed and Turk prepared to open his eyes and resume his approach. Then he noticed a dull thumping sound.

"Hear that?" he whispered to Bates.

"I just hear that damn humming," Bates replied.

"Listen," Turk said. "Close your eyes and listen."

Turk noticed that Bates attempted to steady his breathing. A move, he figured, to help the man better attune himself to the environment.

"Thump, thump, thump," Bates whispered, mimicking the sound that Turk heard over the electrical buzz above them.

Was the thumping getting louder because he was aware of it? Or because it was getting *closer*? He decided if the cause was the latter, he wanted the team in formation and ready to act.

Turk motioned for the rest of the SEALs to join him and Bates. The men moved into position. Together, they approached the corner. Turk squatted and eased himself past the wall. The barrel of his submachine gun left the safety of the concrete barrier. His head followed. The hallway stood empty. He saw steel handrails mounted against the wall on both sides, about waist high. The rails led to the descending stairwell.

"Let's go," he said.

The SEALs moved down the hallway toward the stairwell, each man's movements in time with the man next to or in front of him, as if they'd choreographed it. They were silent killers. A man could have been standing ten feet away, and they wouldn't have heard Turk and his men approaching. Everything went smooth as butter, thought Turk. At least, it did up until the point when Ruiz started coughing.

"Everyone back," Turk ordered.

The team retreated to the far end of the hall, splitting into two groups. One went right, the other left. They faced each other and waited.

"Who did that?" Turk said.

Ruiz stepped forward, his head hanging, eyes cast down at the floor.

"Ruiz?" Turk said. "You alerted anyone down there to our presence. You realize that, right? Or are you the damn FNG now?" Turk brought his right hand to his face and squeezed the bridge of his nose. "You're leading the damn way now, Ruiz."

"Yeah, I got it," Ruiz said.

Turk motioned for the group to get ready as Ruiz stepped past him. He noticed that sweat soaked the man's short spiky black hair and face. He looked over the men nearest to him and saw that they also had sweat on their foreheads. He didn't find the temperature in the facility uncomfortable, but the airflow left a lot to be desired. Plus, nerves were racked, with some men more than others.

Ruiz led the team down the hall toward the stairs. Turk and Bates followed close behind, with the rest of the group in formation behind them. The thumping grew louder the closer they got to the stairwell. The noise rose loud enough that it drowned out the constant buzzing. Turk thought the banging sounded more like a soft thud the closer they got.

They reached the edge of the stairwell and Turk whistled for Ruiz to stop, then he moved up to take position next to the man. There were a dozen stairs that connected to a wide platform. He leaned forward and looked over the inside railing. He saw another set of stairs heading down on the other side of the platform, heading in the opposite direction.

Turk turned and faced his team. “Bates, Schmitty, Spencer,” he said. “You three with me. Ruiz, your ass is going first.” He looked at the man out of the corner of his eye, but saw no discernible reaction. He wondered if Ruiz was even paying attention to what he was saying. “The rest of you, wait until we clear the platform, then head down. I don’t know what’s after the next set of stairs, but if it’s a wall or a door, we’ll all meet there. If it’s open, we’ll figure it out after twelve more steps.”

He turned and nudged Ruiz in the back, sending the man toward the first step. Ruiz hunched over, extending the barrel of his M4 in front of him, began descending the stairs. He took a step, then stopped, presumably to listen. Then he took another step. He stopped twice more before descending the remainder of the stairs to the landing. Despite the speed at which he traveled, he remained silent.

Turk and the three men with him moved without hesitation. They reached the bottom, and the five SEALs leaned against the outer wall. Turk looked over his shoulder at the rest of his team and saw five faces staring back in anticipation. He crouched, approached the other side of the landing. The banging was louder and continued to intensify as he moved past the barrier the stairs had created.

“What am I seeing?” he muttered to himself. He gestured with his head for Ruiz to join him. He wasn’t going to send him ahead again, though. Ruiz had served his punishment for potentially ruining their cover, and Turk wasn’t going to place the man in a situation where he could be killed without backup to watch out for him.

Turk stayed low, Ruiz remained high. They moved in unison past the relative safety of the stairs that shielded them.

There, on the next landing, facing away from them, Turk saw the source of the incessant banging.

Chapter 9

The old man lifted his hands in the air, aimed his pistol toward the ceiling. Sean could tell it was a small-caliber weapon, and felt certain that the bullet wouldn't be able to penetrate his body armor. Plus, the man didn't appear to be the type that would resort to using deadly force. However, Sean had learned long ago not to trust appearances. Why hadn't the man retreated back into the room behind the command room?

"How did you guys get in here?" the old man asked in a thick eastern European accent.

Sean looked at Karl, who didn't appear interested in answering questions.

"Please," the old man said, "I've been trapped in here for ten days. If you got in, that means we can get out. Right? Can we get out?"

"We're not going anywhere," Sean said. "At least, not yet."

The old man nodded and started to take a step back.

"Stop right there, Pops," Karl said. "Step forward and move to that corner." Karl gestured with his head to the corner of the back wall, furthest from the door. "Leave the door open."

The old man complied. He took two steps forward, then sidestepped toward the other side of the room. He made sure to keep the pistol pointed at the ceiling. The look on his face was a mixture of anxiety and excitement. Perhaps he believed they were there to rescue him. Was this the guy who had reached out for help? A shiver ran down Sean's spine at the next thought he had. Did someone in the U.S. government or military know about this guy?

"This far enough?" the old man asked when he reached the corner of the room.

"You can't go any further, can you?" Karl said.

"Suppose not," the old man said.

"Ryder, cover me," Karl said as he started toward the old guy, his MP7 aimed at the man's head. "All right, Pops, lower that arm to the side till it's parallel with the ground."

The man did as he was told. His thin arm shook as he held it perpendicular to his body, locked straight at the elbow, his wrist angled so that the gun pointed toward the ceiling.

Karl approached slowly and cautiously. Sean figured that the SEAL had seen enough, as Sean himself had, to tell him that everyone was a threat inside, and sometimes outside of, hostile territory. A ten-year-old kid could kill you as fast as a trained operative could. Maybe not as gracefully, but he'd kill you all the same. An old man could, too.

Karl reached out and took the pistol from the man. He tucked it away and then turned the guy around, patted him down. Said, "He's clear."

The old man turned around, slowly. "I'm not here to hurt anyone. I just want to go home."

"Yeah, well, don't we all," Karl said.

Sean stepped forward. "Karl, why don't you go check out whatever's behind that door?"

"What if those *things* are down there?"

"Then I doubt he would have been able to come up."

Karl appeared to study the old man for a moment as if the answer were written on the guy's face, then he hiked his shoulders in the air an inch or two and nodded. "Yeah, guess so." He took one last look at the old man, then walked toward the other side of the room.

Sean waited until Karl slipped past the open doorway, then he turned his attention back to the man. “Why don’t you sit down?” He gestured toward the seat in front of him, which was also in front of a working computer. He figured the man to be a technician of some sort, maybe one who knew where to find hidden information within the computer’s file system.

The old guy took a deep breath and exhaled loudly, then walked toward Sean. “You aren’t going to kill me, are you?”

“I don’t think so,” Sean said. “Don’t give me a reason, though.”

The old guy’s lips lifted at the edges, wrinkling the paper thin skin on his cheeks and crumpling his eyes. He stood motionless for a few seconds before sitting down, his face crinkled like used wrapping paper.

“Who are you?” the old man asked.

“I’m an Air Force PJ,” Sean said. “So is that guy over there.” He pointed toward Jules, who was leaned back in a chair with his eyes closed.

The smile on the old man’s face retreated and he looked somber. “What about the other guy?”

“He’s a Navy SEAL.” Sean studied the man for a moment, waiting for a reaction, then continued. “There’s a team of SEALs here. They’re checking out the lower levels now.”

The old man shook his head. “They shouldn’t do that. Can you call them and get them back up?”

“We’re on radio silence. For now. I’m only calling if my life is in danger, and best I can tell, it’s not at the moment.” He offered up a smile, but the old man didn’t react. Sean waited a minute, then asked an obvious question. “Why shouldn’t they be down there?”

“It’s... it’s not safe down there,” he said. “Anywhere in here, for that matter. Except for maybe this room. But even then, for how long?” He looked past Sean and his eyes settled on Jules, then he added, “Judging by your partner, it’s not safe outside, either.”

“Care to tell me why?”

The old guy said nothing. His eyes drifted to the opposite corner of the room.

"Look," Sean said. "You can talk to me, or the SEALs will make you talk. Understand? They have ways to get you to speak if they feel you have information. I'm a PJ. I fix people. Those guys kill people." He lifted an eyebrow and lowered his head. "Now, considering you're the only person we've run into who isn't dead or howling or screaming, the consensus will be that you can provide us with some intel. So why don't you start talking?"

The old man brought his withered hands to his face and pressed his palms into his eyes. Blue veins rose against his flesh and snaked along the backs of his hands and wrists. Brown spots dotted the skin on his arms.

"Where to begin?" he said, shaking his head.

"What's your name?" Sean said.

The man smiled and nodded. "That's a good place to start, I suppose. My name is Richard Knapp." He paused to clear his throat. "Doctor Richard Knapp."

Sean noticed that Knapp held his chin an inch higher as the man added *Doctor* to his name, and he wondered if perhaps Knapp was famous in some circles. He decided to bring him back down to the ground.

"Never heard of you," Sean said.

The man looked disappointed for a moment, then lifted his eyebrows and puffed his cheeks as he forced a large breath out. "Most people haven't, but the ones that have, consider me a legend in the field of—"

"I don't care about all that," Sean said. "Here's what I want to know. What purpose does this building serve? What are those *things* inside of here and roaming around outside of the building? Where the fuck are the Rangers and guys from Delta Force?"

Knapp steepled his fingers together, rubbed his chin with his thumbs. His mouth opened three times, but he didn't say anything. He jerked his head to the side at the sound of footsteps. Karl had reentered the room, and it seemed to have startled Knapp. The man straightened up in his chair while watching the SEAL cross the room and come to a stop next to Sean.

"What's going on?" Karl asked.

"Dr. Knapp here was about to give us some information," Sean said. "What did you find down there?"

"Doctor, huh? Whatever. It's a bunker. Stocked to the hilt. He probably could've lasted three years in here."

Sean turned toward the doctor, saw the man nodding in response to Karl's assumption. "Anyone else down there?"

Karl opened his mouth to answer, however, Knapp cut him off.

"No," Knapp said. "I was the only one fortunate enough to be in this room when *it* happened."

"When what happened?" Sean said.

The old man sighed. "You asked what this place is. Well, simply put, it is a research facility. A biological research facility, to be exact."

Sean had a feeling he knew where this was going, but remained patient and let Knapp tell him in his own words.

"As you can tell," Knapp said, "this place is pretty well hidden. I'd think that if all these different military groups hadn't been by recently, you might not have even noticed it. I'm not sure how those initial men got in here. Wish they hadn't, though. They really set *them* off down below."

"Them?" Karl said.

Sean placed his hand on Karl's forearm, shook his head. "Let him continue."

"Yes," Knapp said. "Them. Anyway, when it happened ten days ago, we were operating on a skeleton crew. One man slipped and hit the wrong button. Instead of securing the cells, he leaves an entire cell block unlocked."

Sean thought back to the diagrams he'd seen of the floors below. He imagined that the big rooms in the corners were what Knapp was referring to when he said cell block. Were the remaining Rangers and members of Delta Force in one of those cells?

"So a group of them got out before I could hit the alarm," Knapp said. "One of them, perhaps one who wasn't completely gone, or changed if you will, had noticed what the guard did and he repeated the process for the remaining cells on the floor. It wasn't long before they made their way to this floor, and who knows where else by this point."

"What are they?" Sean said.

"Humans. Or, they were. Now, they're an experiment gone horribly, horribly wrong."

"This is a research facility for biological warfare, isn't it?" Sean said. "You were..."

Knapp's eyes glistened and he turned away for a moment. When he looked back, he stared at the floor between Sean and himself. "I was forced to come here against my will some years ago. I don't want to go into details about it."

"Someone threatened your life?" Sean said.

The man snorted. "I'd gladly let them take my life if it meant I had never created such a beast."

"They threatened your wife and kids," Karl said.

Knapp looked up with a quick and decisive nod. "Said I had to come here and build them a super-virus. One that could wipe out a population and blow itself out just like that." He snapped his fingers for emphasis. "Our first attempt went fairly well. Over a ninety percent fatality rate." He smiled as if he had unlocked some achievement by killing nine out of ten people.

"What did you test on?" Sean asked, afraid of the answer.

"Humans," Knapp said. "Criminals, mostly. The problem we found in our first attempt was that when new individuals were introduced toward the end of someone's life, they became infected. The virus remained contagious for far too long. That chance that it would cause a global pandemic and send the world to its doom was too great. We were looking at a possible reduction of over ninety percent of the world's population, and that wouldn't cut it."

"Glad to see you maintained an ethical approach," Sean said. "So what did you do? You said we. Are there more like you working on this?" Sean asked.

"Yeah, a couple. Well, they were, but they're gone now." Knapp paused a beat to dab at the tears forming in the corner of his eyes. "Anyhow, we went back to work is what we did. I had been working with H1N1—"

"Swine flu," Karl interrupted.

Knapp's eyebrows rose and he nodded. "The mutation was great, as I said, but it didn't kill itself fast enough. We need the contagious aspect of the virus to die once the cells have been sufficiently attacked, which is something that doesn't take long. You see, it's not a big window, but for most of the areas of the world, population centers, it was plenty of time to spread from person to person and make its way outside of the community."

"It'd have to do that in something like two minutes," Karl said. "No way you could be successful. The world is too connected now."

Knapp smiled. "This would have been a multi-phase attack. I can assure you that if we had been successful, the virus would have only spread so far after each, um, distribution."

"How?" Karl said.

Knapp shrugged. "In some places by force, not allowing people to leave. In other spots by the sheer logistical aspect of it. Time and distance, that sort of thing. They'd never release it on their own soil, that's for sure."

Sean thought about the beings they had encountered outside and in the building, and wondered if Knapp had been successful in completing the next phase of his project. "So what did you do?"

"I tried a few avenues and began working with the rabies virus and variola."

"What's variola?" Karl asked.

"Smallpox."

"But most of the world is vaccinated against smallpox," Karl said.

"Ah, but I create mutations of the microbes that cause the viral infection, and then mutate them even further. I've isolated strands and pulled pieces from here and there and created what I believed to be the ultimate virus for destroying a community of people. It'd blow in and out in a matter of hours, limiting transmissions between hosts and reducing the chances of spread. Say that somehow someone got on a plane to travel overseas or across a country. Well, by the time the plane landed, everyone would be infected, but no one would be contagious." He leaned back against the edge of the workstation. "That's what I'd hoped, at least."

"You can't stop human contact," Karl said. "I hope to God this was meant to be a last resort."

"Those *things* we've seen," Sean said. "They were infected?"

"Yes," Knapp said. "I prefer to say afflicted. Infected sounds treatable."

"We've encountered several. How does this start? I mean, how do you know someone is infected, or afflicted?"

"Coughing, sneezing, fever, fatigue—although I should add that the beings you encountered had been infected long enough that the virus would not have been contagious, unless they inflicted a wound which involved the transfer of bodily fluids."

Sean nodded, thankful that he had not been bitten by one of those *things*. "Then what?"

"Pain, lots of physical pain. You might see uncontrolled movements, an inability to swallow, and there may be sores on the face and hands. The skin seems to lose color. The afflicted may become delusional and hallucinate. Finally, inflammation takes hold, and here's where it gets tricky. Basically, the cells of an organ are attacked until they swell and burst and die."

"Why tricky?" Karl asked.

"Well," Knapp said, "when it is the heart or kidneys or lungs affected, the result is death, and not always immediately. But death, nonetheless. However, and this is only an educated guess because I haven't been able to study it thoroughly, when the brain is attacked, these... mutations occur."

Sean allowed his mind to process the information. He fell back into a chair and looked between Karl and Knapp. Jules coughed in the background, and Knapp pushed off of the desk and looked at him.

"Your friend is infected," Knapp said.

Sean noticed Karl clutch his gun a little tighter and push the barrel away from his chest.

"Bullshit," Sean said. "He's got the flu."

Knapp walked along the back wall and pointed at a wide screen mounted to it. "From these screens I watched the progress of the virus as it attacked our test subjects." He turned and faced the men. "Look at your partner. See how he sweats in reaction to his core temperature rising? See how his skin, once I assume a healthy brown, is turning gray and ashen? Was he attacked by one of them?"

Sean swallowed hard, taking note of how dry his mouth and throat had become. *An inability to swallow*. The words of the scientist echoed in his brain. Panic tore through his body as he feared that he had become infected. He shook his head, stood, walked toward Jules.

"We encountered one up close," Sean said. "Me and Jules did, after we landed. It came out from the bushes and, it looked like it went through him, but it didn't hurt him, only knocked him over. I shot it, then he did, and it died."

"Are you sure it didn't attack him?" Knapp said.

Sean looked Jules over and noticed a thin line of red seeping through the arm of his friend's shirt. He pulled out his knife and cut the sleeve near the shoulder and tore it so that it ripped apart. A thick white bandage stained with blood covered Jules's bicep.

Sean thought back to the night before. The thing had charged past Jules on its way toward him. As it stood before Sean, its mouth hung open, and he recalled seeing strands of saliva. Only it hadn't been saliva, it had been Jules's blood strung between the afflicted's teeth. It had bitten Jules as it had passed by the man.

Sean reached for the bandage.

"I wouldn't touch that," Knapp said. "He's infected."

Sean straightened, backed up. "Does that mean he's been transmitting every time he coughed?"

Knapp nodded. "Afraid so. Up to a point, at least. Like I said, the virus moves past a point of contamination."

"We're all infected?" Sean said.

The scientist shrugged. "There's an incubation period that lasts anywhere from two to twenty-four hours, usually on the shorter end of that spectrum. Has anyone shown symptoms similar to a cold or flu?"

Sean thought about it, but couldn't be sure whether anyone had or not. He shrugged and offered an *I don't know* gesture.

Knapp started to walk toward the open doorway in the back wall. "Well, I think I should return to my room seeing as how you won't be rescuing me. I'm afraid you might try to kill me, if you don't die, that is."

Sean pulled his M9 and aimed it at the man's head. He walked to the door, slammed it shut. "You aren't going anywhere, old man. You created this, you can cure it."

"I'm afraid it's not that simple," Knapp said. "The virus mutated beyond my control, and I have reason to believe that it continues to do so."

Sean grimaced as he stifled a yell. A moment later, he said, "Tell me about mortality rates."

"This is all extrapolation, understand. I don't have accurate numbers. But on a global scale," Knapp looked up to the right as if he was performing calculations in his head, "I'd estimate that ninety-nine point five percent of the world's population would succumb to the virus, with approximately nine in ten dying. That is if it were unleashed."

"And the other one in ten?" Karl asked.

"I believe you've encountered them already."

"What about the point five percent who don't succumb?" Sean asked.

"Those are the ones who are somehow immune. We've seen it down here. Of course in this environment, they are killed by the one in ten afflicted who go on to mutate. So it could be that the point five takes longer to show symptoms." Knapp paused. "I believe they are immune to the initial virus. Would they succumb to another strain, or after being attacked, I can't be sure since none them ever survived the attacks of the deranged beings down below."

Sean grabbed a chair and placed it ten feet away from Jules. He then sat down, facing his friend, who leaned back in a chair, unconscious. Jules's body began to convulse.

"What can you tell us about them?" Karl asked. "I mean, we know we have to shoot them in the head to kill them. But what else?"

Knapp nodded and seemed to contemplate the question. "I don't necessarily think shooting them in the head is required for their death. It's that they are able to tolerate significant pain because their brains have been, for lack of a better word, destroyed. Maybe damaged makes more sense. On the one hand, they are primal beings, and the *human* part of their brains, that which gives them what you might call a soul, is all but lost. But I have noticed some interesting things when watching them. Some of them seem to follow a sort of social structure, if you will. Not all, mind you. There are outliers who are loners. But there are also weaker ones, ones who seem adverse to killing, and a few who seem to hold on to some thread of humanity."

"Outside," Sean said, "there was a woman. One of those afflicted, but clearly a woman. And she hung out by the graveyard." He looked at Knapp, but saw no notice of recollection on the man's face.

"What graveyard?"

“If you’re looking down at the entrance from the hill, it’s to the left.”

“I’m not aware of any graveyard there.”

“There’s mounds, fresh dirt, dozens of them.”

“Interesting,” Knapp said. “No, this is fascinating. They are burying the others, the ones who don’t make it. Tell me, when they—”

Sean held a hand in the air. “I’m not through.”

“Okay.”

Sean got to the point. “How do they move so fast?”

Knapp nodded. “I’ve seen that, too. Both on the screens and in the halls. It doesn’t seem to happen to all of them, though. It seems when they have a purpose, they are capable of moving quite fast. I attribute that to mutations in the muscular system. Not only can they run faster, but they cover more distance with each step. But, without being able to study a body with the purpose of looking for that, I don’t know for sure.”

“Who else knows about this place?” Sean said. “Not knows it’s here. I mean, who knows what goes on here?”

Knapp shrugged as he looked from Sean to Jules. He said, “Your friend is waking up.”

Chapter 10

Her hair rose upward like a puff of steam, pluming with every forward jerk of her head. It hovered for a moment, then cascaded down across her shoulders and back. Soft and blond, it looked like fine silk or satin. Rivers of blood flowed down the concrete wall from the point of her forehead's impact. It gathered into a puddle on the floor, growing thicker and wider by the second. Her gown was ripped down the middle, between her shoulder blades to the hem. Hanging open, it revealed pale skin covering her back and ass and legs. Clusters of black and purple and blue marks spotted her body. Her hands hung by her sides, clenching into fists with each successful meeting between flesh and bone and concrete.

"Miss?" Turk said.

He felt the eyes of his men fall upon him, burning a hole into his back. He didn't know why he spoke. He could tell she was one of *them*, one of those *things*. But she didn't appear to be a threat, much like the woman Sean had pointed out to him in the graveyard. She was a poor soul who somehow ended up in the wrong place at the wrong time, and had her humanity torn from her fleshy cage.

"Miss?" he said again, louder.

The woman stopped and took a step back. Blood trickled into the bare gray spots on the concrete floor where the soles of her feet had been. She turned her head to the left. The skin on her forehead was shredded and bloodied, her skull crushed inward. Crimson liquid covered her eyelids, stained her cheeks, dripped off her chin onto her chest and shoulders. She shuffled in a semi-circle, lifting her feet an inch or two at a time, until she faced Turk and the rest of the men. Her hands rose to her face and clumsily wiped the blood from her eyes, smearing the thick fluid that had begun to cake on her cheeks.

She let out a noise like a moan as her arms fell to her side. Her eyes were bright brown, but distant. She looked at the men, yet right through them as if she saw something else. Something beyond her reach. Perhaps a memory of her old life, thought Turk. Or maybe he and his team didn't appear like humans to her. Maybe not to any of those *things*. Did they look evil to her? And if so, was she perhaps figuring out how to kill them?

He'd seen how fast some of those *things* could move, and began to anticipate her coming toward him.

She groaned a little louder, and it appeared as though her eyes began to water. A tear pooled and fell across her cheek, mixing with some of the thinner blood before falling to the floor, leaving a pinkish trail in its wake. She held out her hands, palms up, thumbs out. Her head tilted to the side. Her mouth dropped open, revealing red gums and cracked, stained teeth.

"What does she want?" Ruiz said.

"To die," Turk said. He lifted his MK 14 and aimed at the woman's head. The right corner of her mouth twitched upward and the glow in her eyes intensified. He wondered if she realized what his intentions were, and if so, did she consider it a favor. He cast all thoughts aside and took a deep breath. Then, he pulled the trigger. The bullet tore through her head, blowing out the back of her skull and scattering bone and brain and more blood onto the wall behind her. Her body remained upright for a moment before collapsing to the floor.

No one spoke. Killing an unarmed woman was not something any of the men set out to do that day. But was it really a woman anymore?

From what they'd seen, one of those *things* could take a man down in under a second. She had to be killed. There was no question about that.

"Come on," Turk said reluctantly.

He took the stairs, caring a little less about how much noise he made. The landing butted up to a solid concrete wall and another set of stairs descended in the opposite direction. He imagined the ceilings on the next floor would be high. Or maybe, the ceiling itself was extra thick. This building could have been around for a while, and perhaps was a fallout shelter at some point. For who, though? There wasn't anyone near here. No major cities, or small ones, for that matter.

Twenty-four stairs later they stood in front of a reinforced steel door. On the other side of the landing was another set of stairs. Turk thought back to the blueprints for the third floor, and he knew that's where those steps led. He hoped to be descending them soon, but first they had to clear the room that hid behind the door.

They had to enter the second floor.

The humming sound that had been present their entire stay now seemed to rise through the stairwell. Turk looked up at the fluorescent light fixture attached to the underside of the landing above. The bulb winked yellow and white at him. He looked from the fixture, to the ceiling, to the wall. Four lines of crimson fluid seeped through the gap between the steel landing above and the concrete wall.

Collins and Brady managed to get the door unlocked around the same time Turk decided to forget about the woman he'd killed moments ago.

"It's ready, Turk," Collins said.

"All right, listen up," Turk said. "I don't have any grand illusions that we're going to find our guys behind this door. Not alive, at least." Fear rose like bile inside him, and he took a moment to compose himself. There was comfort in knowing that he was surrounded by some of the finest soldiers he'd ever had the opportunity to serve alongside. "You need to be quick, and quiet, and decisive. I'd like to say we can take our time and identify whether or not our targets are hostile. We can't, though. If it ain't dressed in ACUs, blow its fucking head off."

No one argued. They all nodded. Each man seemed to understand, or perhaps accept, that they were dealing with something their training had never prepared them for. How could it?

"On my signal," Turk said.

He lifted his hand, gave the command. The team entered the room and split to the left and right, staying close to the wall. The first thing that hit Turk was the stench. The room smelled rotten, a mixture of decomposing bodies and feces. He heard men stifle the bile that rose in their throats as they adjusted to the smell of death.

After the burning in his eyes and nose subsided, Turk realized that the room was dimmer than rest of the building. It seemed that one out of every five lights had been smashed or simply no longer worked. His eyes adjusted to the dark setting and he began to make out shapes, most of which were scattered along the floor. Bodies, he figured, dead bodies. The hum from the lighting was faint, but still present. In a way, Turk found it comforting. As long as that hum was there, he'd get out of the place in one piece. Hopefully alive.

The room wasn't exactly as he expected it to be, based on the blueprints. For one, there was no wall running through the center. It was large and open, with four cellblocks, one in each corner. The cells were open air, enclosed on all four sides and on top by thick steel bars. There was one main gate leading to each block of cells. The gates were all open.

After determining that nothing in the room was moving other than the SEAL team, Turk began to cross the floor. He took three steps and slipped, managing to regain his balance without having to place his hand on the floor, and into whatever he'd slipped on. It crossed his mind to shine his light down to check it out, but he decided against it. Better to not know.

After fifteen feet, it became impossible to walk through the room without stepping on a body. This time he did pull out his light and panned it across the floor. The sight repulsed him. The first thing he noticed was that not a single body was left undisturbed. In some cases, faces were missing, torsos had been ripped open, entrails strung about, flesh torn from various body parts. There were a few that had bullet holes in their foreheads. Presumably they were the beings they'd seen scattered about. After he had processed the gruesome sight, Turk began to take note of the clothing they wore. Most of the bodies were clothed in stained gowns, like those they'd seen being worn by the previous beings they'd encountered. A few of the bodies were wearing khaki pants and white or blue pullover shirts. Drop holsters were attached to their thighs and utility belts strapped around their waists. Security, Turk figured. They'd done an awful friggin' job. Finally, he noticed several men with M4s clutched in their dead hands, their bodies clothed in ACUs.

Rangers.

The bodies of the men they'd been sent to rescue. Would they even be able to recover them?

The buzzing sound in the room increased. Were dead lights returning to life? Turk wouldn't argue if they did. At the very least he'd like to collect each man's dog tags to be returned to their families.

"What the...?" one of his men said from behind.

A series of screams and shrieks erupted from across the room.

Turk looked up and swung his flashlight side-to-side, the glow lighting up the darkest recesses of the room.

Dozens of green and blue and brown eyes reflected against the high powered beam.

The screams grew louder.

"Open fire!" Turk yelled.

Chapter 11

Jules wrapped his hands around the chair's armrests, leaned forward and coughed, something he'd been doing more frequently since waking. Sean thought that he'd noticed a few drops of blood mixed in with the man's saliva.

"How're you feeling?" Sean asked.

Jules shook his head. The motion was anything but fluid. His chest and shoulders convulsed. "Not... not so... good." He tried to smile, but his upper lip only managed to jerk up a couple times on the left side of his face.

Sean wanted to approach his friend and comfort him. But he didn't. He was scared. Scared for what Jules was going through, as well as what was to come. Sean was under no delusions that his friend was going to make it out of this alive. He was also frightened by the prospect that in the next few hours, he too might be suffering in the same manner.

Jules fell forward and placed his head between his knees as he coughed. The floor below him became spattered with thick dark mucus and blood. He stopped coughing and pushed off of his knees and lifted his head. Blood that originated from the corner of his eyes dripped down his cheeks. The spasms seemed to have stopped, for the moment at least.

Welcome relief, Sean thought, *if only for a few brief seconds*.

"What's happening to him?" Sean said, looking away from Jules and toward Knapp.

Knapp sighed as he leaned forward in his chair and studied Jules for a moment. "Looks like he's ruptured his sinuses. Now, is that from all the coughing, or the cause of all of it? Does it matter? He doesn't have much time left."

"Give me a real answer," Sean said.

"A real answer." The old man seemed to contemplate humoring Sean. "The microbes are attacking the cells in his body, infesting and feasting on them," Knapp said. "They'll continue to do so until each cell can take no more, at which point it bursts and dies. Judging by the amount of coughing and the blood and mucus, I'd say it's his lungs that are being destroyed."

Sean shook his head, looking between Knapp and Jules, saying nothing.

"I know you don't want to hear this," Knapp said, "but the best thing you can do is take your gun and place it to your friend's head, then pull the trigger."

Sean's eyes welled up at the thought, more so because he had been thinking it himself. He didn't need Knapp to tell him that killing his friend would be the right thing to do. He looked at Jules, and saw the man nodding.

"Do it," Jules whispered between heavy shivers. He brought his hand to his face and wiped across his nose, dragging a thick line of bloody mucus over his cheek. His breathing was ragged and sporadic. "Do it."

Sean stood and unholstered his M9. He stepped forward and extended his arm. He tried to take aim, but his forearm and wrist were shaking and prevented him from lining up an accurate shot. He reached out with his left hand, cupped his right, and steadied himself. Tears blurred his vision, distorting his best friend's face. It wasn't murder, he told himself. At worst, assisted suicide. Jules was dead no matter what. The man lacked the strength or wherewithal to turn his own gun on himself, and therefore relied on Sean to do it for him.

"Get it... over... with."

Sean rotated his head and blinked to clear the tears from his eyes. He took aim and placed his finger on the trigger. The plating was cold against the pad of his fingertip.

"Now!" Jules managed to yell.

Sean let out a guttural scream. "I can't do it." He lowered his weapon to the floor and his head followed.

"Get out of the way," Karl said. "I'll put him out of his misery."

Sean looked up. First thing he saw was Jules straighten his body and lean his head back. The man's lips quivered and rose and fell in a tepid attempt at a smile. His shoulders broadened, then he pulled them back. He was making a target out of himself. Sean knew then that Jules was prepared to die.

Sean felt Karl push past him, a Sig Sauer P226 in his right hand. Karl lifted his arm and took aim at Jules.

"Don't," Sean said. "Don't you fucking shoot him."

"Look at him, Sean. He wants to die."

"Die... want..." Jules said.

"Then I'll do it," Sean said. "I'm his best friend. I'll do it."

Karl turned his head and looked Sean in the eye. He lowered his pistol, letting it hang by his side. "Have at it."

Sean took another step forward, but instead of aiming his side arm at Jules, he pointed it at the scientist.

The old man threw his hands in the air and pushed back in his chair with his legs.

"What can you do for him?" Sean said through clenched teeth.

"Wh-what?" Knapp said.

"I know you can do something for him, old man. What?"

"I-I don't... there's nothing we can do."

"Easy there, Sean," Karl said.

Sean knew that Karl didn't give two craps about Knapp. His primary concern was most likely whether or not Sean had flipped, and if so, how he would deal with it.

"What can I do for him?" Sean said.

The old man shook his head. His eyes locked onto Sean's and he rose from his seat. He took a step forward and waited, presumably to see how Sean would react. When Sean did nothing, the man took another few steps, coming to a stop a few feet in front of him. "I'm sorry. There's nothing that can be done."

"No," Sean said as tears welled in his eyes. "You did this to him. You made this. You have to know how to fix it."

Knapp nodded. "I'm as much of a monster as those *things* that roam the halls, encasing me in this small tomb." His hands gestured through the air around him. "I let things get out of hand, that is true. But know this, if there were a way for me to cure him, I would."

Sean grabbed the man by his collar and pulled him close. He pressed the barrel of his gun under the scientist's cheek, jamming it tight to the bone. Knapp's eyes grew wide and he stuttered, but couldn't get a word out.

"One of these," Sean said, "is reserved for you."

He released his grip and pushed the old man back a few feet, never breaking his stare.

"Sean," Karl said.

"What?"

"Look, man. Look at Jules."

Sean blinked and turned toward his partner. The tortured expression on Jules's face had relented. He now looked calm and at peace. Jules lifted his eyelids, revealing eyes that reflected the light around them, glowing with the color of amber. He shut them tight. His deep breaths became ragged and loud.

"What in the name of all that's holy?" Sean said.

Knapp stepped forward, stopping within two feet of Jules. He leaned over and inspected the man. Jules eyes opened wide, causing Knapp to fall backward onto a desktop.

"He's turned," Knapp said. "Oh my God, he's turned. Kill him. Do it now!"

Karl brought his arms up and extended his pistol. "You better do this Sean, or I'm going to."

Sean walked up to his friend and knelt in front of him. He reached out with his left hand, placing it on Jules's shoulder. He gave his friend a reassuring squeeze and a half-smile. Jules returned the smile, closed his eyes, and leaned his head back. He looked at peace, something that Sean was sure would fade soon as Jules transformed further into one of the afflicted.

Sean rose and walked around the chair. He placed the barrel of his gun against the back of Jules's head. Then, closing his eyes and reciting a prayer he learned as a child, Sean pulled the trigger and ended his best friend's life.

The shot echoed throughout the room and the smell of cordite filled Sean's nose, causing him to cough in an attempt to flush the smell and taste from his mouth.

"I'll move him," Karl said, already pushing Sean out of the way. Karl lifted his right arm and coughed into the crook of his elbow. "Hope I'm not coming down with this." He smiled at Sean. "If I am, there better be someone else around to kill me. You take too damn long."

Sean smiled, unsure of the reason why. He tried to convince himself that it wasn't Jules he'd killed. Jules was gone, replaced by a monster.

"It had to be done," Knapp said. His tone was sharp, and his speech curt.

"No," Sean said. "It didn't. It's because of you it had to be done. It's because of you that these beings wander the halls and the area outside, lost and confused, full of deranged thoughts leading them to kill. It's because of you that U.S. soldiers are dead."

"Don't take that tone with me," Knapp said. "You sons of bitches, Americans, you did this to yourself. Who do you think funds this place? Nigeria? Get over yourself, man. You brought this upon yourself."

Sean lunged and extended his hands. His palms lifted the old man by his chest and he hoisted him into the air and threw him against the wall. Knapp's body hit with a thud and fell to the floor, causing him to land on his side. He yelled in pain, then groaned.

Sean rushed up to him. "What's in your pocket?"

Knapp looked up while feeling around for his glasses. He found them, and then placed them on his head.

Sean started feeling around Knapp's shirt and chest. He'd felt something in his shirt pocket. Something hard. Was the old guy carrying another weapon, waiting for the right moment to use it?

"Get away from me," Knapp yelled as he fought and clawed against the intrusion.

Sean wrapped his left hand around Knapp's collar, then balled his right hand into a fist. He struck the old man across the face. Knapp's body went limp. Sean reached inside Knapp's breast pocket and pulled out a syringe, capped on the end. He held it out in front of him, stretched across both palms. He couldn't tell if it was empty or full, so he stood and walked over to stand underneath the brightest light. Tilting each end of the syringe up then down, he saw fluid moving inside the tube.

The doctor sat with his back against the wall, watching Sean.

"What's in this syringe?" Sean said.

Knapp shook his head.

Sean aimed his gun at the man, noticing that bits of blood, skull and hair were stuck to the end of the barrel. "Tell me."

"It's an antidote," Knapp said, lowering his eyes. "The only one left. There's a couple doses in there at most."

Sean felt the room start to spin, and his knees went weak. He could have saved Jules if only he'd pressed Knapp harder. But he didn't. He'd murdered Jules when his life could have been spared. He steadied himself by placing his left hand on the back of a chair. Then he reached down with his right and retrieved his M9.

"You son of a bitch," he said as he lifted his arm and aimed the gun at Knapp's head. He didn't bother to steady himself, or to think it over. He simply pulled the trigger.

Chapter 12

The bullet tore through his forehead, ripping off half of his skull. His body bowed backward into the wall, then folded over itself as it fell to the floor, leaving behind a silhouette of blood and brain and bone.

"Got you, you bastard," Turk yelled.

All around him bullets flew from the barrels of the SEALs' MK 14 EBRs and their HK MP7 submachine guns. Turk watched the advancing line of the beings, picking off the ones that broke from the ranks and charged them. For some reason, they moved at a slow pace while crossing the room. He presumed that not all of them had the ability to move as quickly. But in a group as large as the one they faced, there had to be at least a few. Was it because of the bodies that littered the floor, blocking a clear path? That had to be it. They couldn't cross the distance because of all the debris, if you could call the fleshy shells that a soul once occupied debris. He then recalled that one had tried, but tripped and crashed to the floor. It was the act of falling that had caught Turk's attention, and now he knew that was because he hadn't seen it move from the wall to the body because it had covered the distance in no time at all.

He noticed several of their shots were hitting the things in their chests. While not an ideal shot, it did slow them down even further and caused additional congestion within their ranks. As they bodies piled up, the shots became easier to pull off. Turk didn't have to readjust his sights as much in order to line up his shot. He'd hit one and it'd go down and the next would be right behind the one he'd wounded or killed a moment before. He took a moment to survey the line and saw the other SEALs were operating in much the same manner as him.

The beings weren't organized. If they had managed to work together, it wouldn't have even been a match. Close to a hundred of them and only ten SEALs. With the speed and power those *things* possessed, Turk estimated they should have been able to kill half of them, at most. But now there were only a couple dozen left.

He continued to pick them off, one at a time. Tall, short, fat, thin. It didn't matter to him. He killed indiscriminately, like they did. He remained calm when he had to reload, as did his men. Every time they did, the line of beings advanced a little further. Despite that, the SEALs maintained control and stayed focused on the task at hand. Maybe they hadn't been trained for this exact scenario, but their training prepared them to handle anything and to think outside the box. That skill was necessary now more than ever.

Turk noticed the remaining beings changed tactics. They had been shuffling through the bodies, dragging their feet on the ground and pushing the corpses around. One stepped up and stood on top of a body. Not an easy task for the clumsy being. It bounced around a few times before settling in.

Turk took aim, but not before he caught a glimpse of the other afflicted doing the same. He squeezed the trigger, perhaps a second too soon, and shot the being in the shoulder. It jerked back, then squared up. Before Turk could fire again, the guy was right in front of him, reaching for Turk's gun.

Turk pulled back and fell to the floor. He yelled, but knew that amid the gunfire, no one would hear him. The being held the barrel of his weapon, and no matter how hard Turk tugged, its grip would not loosen. Turk angled the gun, then fired. The round entered underneath its chin and blew out the top of its head.

Turk scooted back until he found the wall. He used it to help him get to his feet. He saw four of his men falling back, firing wildly at the remaining beings who huddled together around the other five members of his team. The group had all charged at the same time and overtook the five SEALs in the blink of an eye. It was pure luck that they didn't follow the first one through and converge on Turk.

Turk looked back at the surviving men and yelled, "Go! Get your asses out of here."

The gunfire ceased as Brady, Schmitty, Bates and Steele escaped through the door into the stairwell.

The buzzing sound increased as the *things* bit and tore through the flesh of his men, not all of who were dead yet. Turk heard their pained screams and cries for help. Ruiz's head poked out from the pile of carnage. His eyes were open, staring right at Turk. His mouth was wide, but he couldn't scream.

Turk aimed his rifle and fired, sending a bullet through the top of Ruiz's skull. He kept his sights on the group as he walked backward toward the stairwell door, firing every few steps. One of his men flung the door open as he approached. Turk turned and ran the remaining distance.

They huddled together behind the closed door. The stairwell, though open and far from safe, provided them with respite from the feeding frenzy going on in the room.

"We're gonna open that door and we're gonna kill the rest of those damned *things* and send them back to hell," Turk said. "If you don't think you can do it, then turn your gun on yourself right now."

He didn't wait for them to respond. Turk ripped the door open and stepped back into the room. Stopped. Aimed. Fired. He heard the other four men do the same. One by one they picked off the feasting beings. The afflicted didn't even stop to see why their fellow beings were falling to the ground. The final shots were fired and the last one fell. The hush that fell over the room was matched in intensity only by the heavy odor of cordite.

Turk scanned the area, looking for signs of life, whether human or *them*. Nothing moved. But, for the first time, he noticed a faint trace of light from the other side of the room, in front of the cell block.

"You guys see that?" he said.

"Yeah," Bates said. "Is that...?"

"Come with me," Turk said. "Rest of you, cover us. Anything moves, kill it. Don't second guess. Shoot."

Turk remained close to the wall, rubbing his left shoulder against it. The perimeter of the room, for some reason, had remained clear. Battle was chaotic. He supposed random chance could have intervened and left the bodies in the center of the room. However, his gut told him that someone had moved the bodies that had fallen on the outer perimeter of the room, sweeping them toward the center. *Just like trash,* he thought.

The humming increased in intensity as they once again approached the light source. He saw a five foot wide by fifteen foot long grate in the floor. Rebar crisscrossed the opening, leaving four or five inch gaps.

"Jesus H. Christ," Turk said.

"Is that...?" Bates said.

Turk nodded, taking in the sight of seven men dressed in ACUs, trapped in the corner of the room below, protected from a horde of those *things* by a few steel bars.

"Can we reach them from here?" Bates asked.

Turk leaned forward and placed his hands on his knees. "Even if we could, they're surrounded by steel on all four sides *and* on the top. We'd have to figure out how to open the cage to get them out."

"Look at all them down there," Bates said, pointing at the masses of beings that stood shoulder to shoulder with their gazes fixed on the men in the cage. "No way we can wade through that shit."

Turk knew this was true, but he also realized that they had the perfect vantage point to thin out the group. "We can start shooting them from here. If our guys down there can open the cell, maybe they can make a break for it."

"There's too many of those damn *things*, Turk," Bates said. "We don't have the ammunition."

"Then we'll get some," Turk yelled. "We'll get another damn team out here."

Bates shook his head. "Let's go before we all end up dead, or worse." His eyes scanned the sea of afflicted below them.

"We're not leaving them here," Turk said. "Not like this. Not surrounded by those creatures."

Bates said nothing. He didn't even bother to look at Turk while the team leader yelled at him. And with good reason, Turk saw as he followed the man's stare. Not only had Bates heard him loud and clear, so had most of the beings below them. They stood with their heads back, arms lifted up, mouths agape, staring up at the two men.

"You want some of this," Turk yelled at them. "Come get it."

He stuck the barrel of his gun through one of the openings between the rebar and began shooting. Every shot penetrated a forehead, and the beings either dropped, or fell against the others, sandwiched and unable to fall.

Turk learned something new at that moment. The bastards couldn't only run fast, they could also jump high.

A pale hand wrapped around the rebar, another around the barrel of his gun. He felt the gun pulled through the opening until it reached a spot where the hilt was too wide. Before he could back up, the thing grabbed a hold of Turk's wrist and pulled his right forearm through a gap. He saw its mouth open, yellow teeth glistening with saliva. The beast was hungry, hell, starving after staring at the men in the cell below for so long. No matter how hard Turk pulled back, the thing wouldn't let go.

When he glanced at Bates, he saw the man was lying on his side, his neck wide open and squirting blood. The thing had moved so fast that Turk didn't see it strike the man. Now, it had a hold of him.

He began to think about his wife and two sons. Turk pushed the thoughts from his mind as they would only hinder him in this situation. He wouldn't let the decrepit thing on the other side of the grate take his life.

He reached across his body for his side arm. The cool handle met the sweaty flesh of his palm, giving him hope, for a moment, that he'd escape the situation with both his hand and his life. He twisted and took aim. The beast sunk its teeth into Turk's arm before he could get the shot off. Turk screamed in pain and unloaded his magazine into the disfigured face below him.

Chapter 13

"Jesus, Ryder!" Karl yelled. "What're you doing?"

Sean watched Knapp's body slide along the wall to the right, leaving a crimson trail in its wake. He walked up to the corpse and nudged the dead man's shoulder with the tip of his boot, looking for any reaction or sign of life. The old man had created these *things* that wandered the halls and outside the facility. Perhaps he had found a way to turn him into one without the side effects. Still, Sean figured it'd be damn hard for anyone to survive with half of their brain plastered to a wall.

"Ryder," Karl said.

Sean didn't respond. He turned his head toward Jules's body, then back toward Knapp.

"Ryder," Karl said again.

"What?" Sean said.

"We needed him alive, man."

"Sorry," Sean said flatly.

"He probably had more info. Turk would have wanted to talk to him."

Sean turned to face Karl. He cleared his throat, then said, "You think Turk's still alive? When's the last time we heard from him, huh?" He paused and lifted an eyebrow. "We haven't. They walked down into the depths of this place. Straight into the pits of hell. They're gone, Karl. And they left us up here with patient zero." He gestured with his head to the woman who stood outside the room with her forehead pressed against the glass. Then he glanced toward Knapp. "And this old coot."

Karl coughed into his hand, then said, "Look, Sean, I know you're distraught after what happened with Jules. But, —"

"You're sick," Sean said. "You've got it."

Karl's grip on his MP7 tightened as he took a step back, placing himself out of Sean's immediate reach.

"Your skin's changing already," Sean said.

"Jules was sick, I'm sick, and you're probably sick, Sean." Karl paused, perhaps waiting for a reaction. When Sean said nothing, he continued. "But I need you to get it together, man. We need to find Turk and get out of this damn place."

Sean relaxed his grip on his pistol as he considered Karl's words. They only had to get through two sections of hallway to reach the tunnel that led out of the building. It had only taken them so long to reach the command room because they had no idea what lie beyond their position. But now, they'd be hauling ass to get out, after they found Turk of course.

If they tried to find him.

"Turk and the others walked down to their death," Sean said.

"We're all brothers," Karl said.

Sean contemplated this, but did not offer a reply.

"I'm going down there, Ryder. I won't hold it against you if you don't come along."

Sean turned away from Karl and crossed the room. He stopped in front of Jules and lowered his head. That wasn't his friend in front of him. Not the man that he'd spent the better part of the last eight years with, bunking together before Sean and Kathy were married. Jules followed suit shortly after when he found Marie. He knew that their daughters would still play together, and their wives would sit on the porch and chat about whatever it is two married women talk about. But never again would he and Jules share a couple cold beers on a hot August day, talking about nothing at all, while waiting for their next mission. He wished they could have one more conversation, but he knew there was no point in wishing. He had to save himself, and he had to save Turk, because maybe the man had a best friend and a wife and a kid or two at home who needed him. Sean reached out and grabbed Jules's dog tags, snatching them off of his neck. He wiped them on his pants leg, removing the sticky blood, and then placed them in his pocket. There were two tags. One for a wife, and one for a daughter. Both of whom would never see Jules again.

"You with me, Ryder?" Karl asked, now positioned a few feet behind Sean.

Sean had been so lost in his thoughts that he hadn't heard the man approach. "Yeah. Let's go get them, and then get moving."

"Okay. But first, let me scan through the computer one more time. If there's anything on here that can help us, I want to bring it."

Sean nodded. He took one last look at Jules, then turned toward the front of the room. The woman still stood outside, centered between the door and the other end of the room. She leaned forward with her forehead planted against the glass, leaving her body at an angle. Her arms dangled straight down with her fingers spread wide. Blood covered her right hand. Dirt caked her left.

Sean stopped in front of her, about six inches away from the window. The woman's eyes, which had been fixed on nothing, rose to meet his. Her facial expression showed no discernible change as she took in his face. Her eyes didn't narrow, or become duller or brighter. She simply stared at him, into his eyes. But did she really see him? Sean leaned in and placed his forehead against the glass. Their eyes were no more than two inches apart. He noticed tears starting to well up along the bottom of her eyelids. When the thin flap of skin could contain them no longer, they pushed past the corners of her eyes and cut a trail through her dirt smeared cheeks. He wondered what thoughts went through her mind. Hell, did she still have thoughts of the sort that he would be able to comprehend? Was her soul trapped behind that pale, ghastly exterior? Were her tears an effort at communicating with him in a way she could no longer vocalize?

Did an angel lurk behind a demon's exterior?

"Hey, Karl," Sean said.

"Yeah," Karl said.

"You think these are zombies?"

Karl chuckled for a second, then said, "Maybe." He coughed, then cleared his throat before adding, "Hell, who's gonna tell us we're wrong to call them that?"

Sean smiled at Karl's statement. Who could tell him he's wrong? No one, because he was the only one living this nightmare.

"Zombies it is," Sean said.

"I'm not finding much on this computer," Karl said.

Sean wondered if the man had changed the subject on purpose. He looked over his shoulder, then said, "Give up looking for info and see if you can get those monitors working. I'd like to see what we're about to walk into."

Karl said nothing in reply, but a flurry of fingers striking against a keyboard told Sean that the man had been receptive to the idea.

When Sean turned his back toward the window again, he saw that the woman had raised her hands to her shoulders and placed them against the glass. Her palms and the pads of her fingers were lined with cuts and crusted blood. Dirt was packed into a wide gash in her left palm. He thought back to the cemetery and wondered if the dirt on her hand had come from one of the mounds he saw outside the facility. Had she buried a loved one there? Or had she been searching for someone already buried there? Maybe a loved one who now only existed in the recesses of her damaged brain? He had a feeling that the dirt covering her hand perhaps correlated to the sadness that caused the tears that streamed down her face a few minutes earlier.

"Got one," Karl said.

The words bounced around inside Sean's head for a moment before he realized what the man was talking about. He backed away from the window and turned and began scanning the monitors on the wall. The one that hung above Knapp's dead body flickered on and began to show a scene that made Sean's heart skip a beat and his stomach sink.

"I don't know what these codes mean," Karl said.

"Forget them," Sean said. "Look."

The screen zoomed in and out of focus and the lighting went from dark to bright and back to dark again. The picture settled in somewhere in the middle. The monitor displayed a scene out of a horror film. A room full of zombies packed shoulder to shoulder. They swayed, perhaps in rhythm, and they all seemed to be focused on something just off the screen.

"Can you pan around?" Sean asked.

"Let me see," Karl said.

A moment later the picture on the screen started moving, sending the current crop of zombies to the bottom corner of the monitor. When the camera reached the other end of the room, Sean said, "Stop." The scene was the same, but different. The zombies were still packed tight to one another, however a group of them stared upward. He saw one that appeared to be hanging from the ceiling, half of the right side of its head missing, its body limp.

"What is that?" Sean said, inching closer to the monitor. He reached out and pointed to the upper left corner. "Can you zoom in on that area?"

As the camera started to zoom, Sean noticed one of the zombie's head erupt into a cloud of blood.

"Holy shit! Stop!" Sean said.

The picture froze and Sean noticed two things. One, zombies were being picked off one at a time. He saw one flinch and fall, then another. Sometimes their heads erupted. Other times their bodies collapsed. As Sean scanned the monitor, he noticed that behind the cells in the corner were seven faces of men he didn't know, but instantly recognized.

"Good news and bad news," Sean said.

"Good news first," Karl said.

"Turk," Sean paused to wipe his brow, "or someone on your team, is alive and above that floor. They're picking off zombies from up there."

"Bad news?"

"I found the guys from Delta."

"Where?"

"In the back corner of that room."

Karl said nothing.

"Locked in a cage."

"Let's get going," Karl said.

"We need to figure out what to do about her," Sean said.

He turned around, but the woman was gone. He rushed forward and pressed against the glass, trying to look down the hallway to the left and the right. She was nowhere to be seen. They were at a disadvantage since the room was recessed from the hall. After five feet, there was a good portion of the corridor they were blind to. For all Sean knew, the woman waited outside with an army of zombies waiting to tear them apart limb by limb.

"Where'd that bitch go?" Karl said.

"I don't know," Sean said. "Hopefully back outside."

"All right, here's what we're going to do." Karl paused for a moment too long.

"What?" Sean said.

"You're not going to like this."

"What?"

"We need to use Jules as bait."

"What do you mean?"

"Toss him into the hall."

"Hell with that," Sean said. "Use the doctor. They probably hate him and will attack him on sight."

Karl seemed to consider this. His lips worked side to side. His eyebrows rose, and his eyes looked up, as if he was performing some complex calculation in his head.

"Okay," Karl said. "We'll use Knapp. Give me a hand."

Sean grabbed the old man by his legs while Karl scooped him off the floor by placing his arms around Knapp's chest from behind. He wasn't a heavy guy, and it didn't require much effort to carry him to the door. They stopped. Sean dropped Knapp's legs. He reached for the door handle, stopping to take a deep breath before turning the knob.

"Nice and easy," Karl said.

Sean pulled the door open, exercising caution. He had one hand on the knob, the other around the handle of his M9. He'd have preferred his submachine gun at that moment, but felt he had better control with his pistol in this situation. He stopped when the door was open wide enough to push Knapp's body through.

"All right," Karl said. "I'm going to shove him. Get ready to close the door when I'm clear, but leave it open a crack. If she pounces, I'm taking her out. But, you better be ready to back me up in case I don't have time to get her."

Sean nodded. He felt a pang of concern travel through his body, then cast it aside. One way or another they were dead. He was sure of it. He figured they ought to send as many of those damned creatures to hell before he and Karl finally bit it.

Knapp's body hit the floor with a thud and slid about four feet, coming to a stop in the middle of the hall. Sean felt his stomach knot. His heart beat faster than he cared to calculate, knowing it would only serve to send him deeper into panic.

Ten seconds passed, nothing happened. Were these zombies smarter than he anticipated? He was sure she'd pounce the moment the body hit the ground, yet here they were, precious seconds ticking by and nothing happening.

"Okay," Karl said. "Another fifteen seconds and we move."

Sean nodded and began counting down from fifteen. He never reached one.

"Screw it," Karl said. "Let's go."

Karl squeezed through the doorway before Sean could say anything. He found himself rushing to get out of the room. On some level, the decisive action taken by Karl helped Sean. He forgot about his pulse and breathing and the panic that coursed through his veins with every beat of his heart. He couldn't forget the situation they were in, though. Not that he'd want to. At least, not now. To do so would spell death. They had to get out of there alive, and for that to happen, he had to remain alert.

Karl spun to the right. Sean turned his back to the man and scanned the left side of the hallway.

"Empty," Karl said.

"Same here," Sean said.

"Where'd she go?"

"Hopefully she left." Sean meant it, too. He didn't want to have to pull the trigger and watch whatever faint trace of a soul remained in the woman fade from her sorrowful eyes.

"Let's go, Sean," Karl said.

Sean turned and caught up to the SEAL. Tactics were thrown out the window now. They were up against an enemy for which they had no protocol. Some of the zombies moved so damn fast that they'd be on top of them by the time one alerted the other. To get out of this alive, Sean knew that they'd have to shoot first, and forget about asking questions altogether. Still, every ten feet or so, he'd glance over his shoulder, finding it impossible to escape the feeling that they were being watched.

The lights flickered above them. Perhaps the power supply was nearing the end of its dwindling life. Or maybe one of the afflicted was sitting in an electrical room chewing through wires. Sean's hand went to his belt and grabbed hold of the butt of his flashlight. It provided little comfort to him to know that he'd only be able to see a small section of the area in front of him should the lights go out and fail to come back on.

The only noise in the hallway was the constant buzzing that had been prevalent everywhere, except in the command room. He began to wonder if it wasn't the lights, but rather the life that existed within the building that created the sound.

They slowed as they approached the end of the hallway.

Karl turned to Sean and said, "Let's take this real slow. I'll stay high, you go low. We round the corner together."

"Okay," Sean said, turning toward Karl and making eye contact with the man.

If he'd kept his eyes focused in front of him, he would have noticed the bloody hand that wrapped around the corner of the wall. Then it wouldn't have been as much of a surprise when patient zero, the woman on the other side of the control room glass, launched herself straight at him.

Chapter 14

"Get your ass off of me," Turk yelled at the lifeless being whose jaw remained clenched around his arm. He fired again, disregarding his own safety, and landed a shot that severed the right side of the thing's mandible from its head. He pulled his arm up and through the grate, refusing to look at the damage to his forearm. Instead, he took a few steps back and resumed firing. It seemed that not all of the afflicted had the ability to run fast or jump high. Only a select few had that good fortune. The rest milled about and moved at the same speed as the zombies Turk had grown up watching in horror movies.

He stopped shooting for a moment and scanned the crowd below, taking note of the tortured, soulless faces that stared up at him. Their eyes were bright, but hollow. Their skin was pale, discolored. Some of them had serious wounds on their heads and torsos. Their deep and wide gashes were crusted over, and in some cases, looked to be infected.

"Maybe they are zombies," he muttered.

He'd have smiled if he weren't so tired. He turned at the waist and saw his men engaged in combat. Turk shook his head at the decision he had to make. Help them, or continue trying to thin the herd below. He walked the other side of the grate, being careful to stay back should another zombie jump up and reach through for his leg. Once at the other end, he knelt down and lowered his head in an effort to see as far across the room as he could.

Turk found the sight below far from encouraging. The entire room appeared to be packed with zombies. They stood shoulder to shoulder, their eyes fixed on the being in front of them. The zombies closest to the cell block stared at the men in the cages. For the most part, they seemed oblivious to the SEALs above them.

We can't win this, Turk thought. But he couldn't leave the men locked up. Maybe it was time to call in and ask for help. Get the Army to send as many men as they could to come down here and fight the creatures below. He shook his head, knowing they'd laugh him off if he mentioned the word *zombies*. Even if they did take him seriously, how long would it take another company of Rangers to get there? How long had the guys from Delta been in captivity? At least four days from what Turk recalled. Why wasn't he sure? Why couldn't he remember simple details about the mission?

"Turk!"

The scream cut through the stiff, stale air like a hot knife through flesh.

Turk looked up and saw that one of his guys was attacking the others. He called out. Steele turned at the waist. Brady and Bates were on the floor, injured, barely moving. Steele held Schmitty's lifeless body by the neck, a foot off the ground. It appeared that half of Schmitty's face had been ripped off.

Steele smiled. His eyes shone bright. He dropped Schmitty and hunched over.

Turk lifted his rifle and set his sights on Steele's forehead. However, before he squeezed the trigger, Steele lunged to the side and finished off Bates, whose final scream was cut short as Steele buried his face into the man's neck and tore through the flesh, crushing his larynx.

Turk readjusted his weapon, and then fired. The first two shots hit Steele in the side, knocking him over onto his back. The man scooted along the floor, using his elbows to prop himself up, until he reached the wall. He tried to get to his feet, but Turk didn't allow it. He squeezed the trigger one more time, sending a bullet into Steele's forehead. The man's body folded over itself and fell to the floor.

Bates lay still on the floor. Turk didn't have to kneel down and inspect him to know that the man was dead. He turned his attention to Brady, who dragged himself with one arm toward Turk. His left arm was severed above the elbow, and blood pumped out in rhythm with his heart, forming a dark red river in his wake. He stopped and pushed himself up so that his chest was off the ground. Turk did his best to prevent his disgust at the site of the mangled man from showing on his face. One of Brady's eyes was hanging from its socket, and his nose had been severed. Deep gashes lined his right cheek, and the wounds continued through both lips. Turk knew they were severe wounds, but they weren't grave. However, the amount of blood the man had lost, and would continue to lose from his severed arm, was. Turk had to apply a tourniquet if there was any hope of saving Brady's life.

Turk knelt down and started to turn the man over. However, when he saw the damage to Brady's abdomen, he stopped.

"Just stay still," Turk said. He laid Brady's head down to the floor, then stood up. He walked behind the man, stopped, and aimed his rifle at the back of the SEALs head. "Forgive me," he said as he pulled the trigger and ended Brady's life.

He remained still for a moment, looking at the four men he'd served with. All of them had been with him for longer than three years. They'd ate together, trained together, killed together. Now, they'd died together, and he wondered if he'd soon join them.

For the first time, Turk noticed the intense pain in his arm. He flinched at the damage the zombie had inflicted. He laughed when he realized that his mocking them by calling them zombies had become prophetic. *Damn flesh eaters.* He determined that while the wound looked grisly, there wasn't enough constant blood loss to require a tourniquet. He'd worry about cleaning the wound if he escaped the building alive.

Turk grabbed the rifles and submachine guns from his fallen SEALs, then moved back to the grate. He stared down at the remaining members of Delta, trapped in their cages like lab rats. The men stared back with faces devoid of hope. Despite Turk's efforts, the room was packed full of those beings. There was no way he was getting the men out alive.

He slipped his pack off his back and set it on the floor. He reached inside and pulled out a pouch that held two small phones. The first one had no signal. He didn't expect it to considering it was a satellite phone. The cellular phone would be hit or miss, he figured, although cellular communications was not his specialty. He'd had a decent signal outside, so it was a matter of how strong the antenna was, and what the builders of the facility placed in the ground above him. As he waited for the phone to boot up, Turk glanced around the room and, for the first time, noticed a faint trace of light from the corner nearest him. He grabbed his bag, slung it over his shoulder and walked toward the glow.

The light came from a shaft that appeared as though it might reach the surface. The opening was too small to tell if it led into another room in the facility or outside, but it appeared to be the best place to attempt a call. The phone finished booting up and Turk saw that it had a signal. It was faint, but a signal nonetheless. He pressed and held down the number five, sending a call to his CO. The man answered, and Turk began to relay everything that had happened, painting a vivid picture of the scene below him. He felt ridiculous using the word zombie over the phone, and was sure they would have him committed the moment he stepped foot on U.S. soil.

"Sir," Turk said. "I don't know how long those men down there have left. How soon can you get reinforcements here?"

"Stand by, Chief."

Turk clutched the phone and pressed it tight to his ear. He scanned the room, looking for any signs of movement. Everywhere he looked, he saw shadows dance across the floor and the walls. Upon closer inspection, he'd find nothing there. He wondered what the hell was wrong with him. Was it fear? He glanced at the wound on his arm and wondered if something worse than fear was causing his mind to play tricks on him.

"Get out," his CO said abruptly.

"Sir?"

"There are no reinforcements, Turk. They're going to carpet bomb the area. You've got an hour, hour-and-a-half max to get your men and get out of there."

"My men are dead," Turk said. "The guys from Delta, I can't get to them."

"Leave them then."

"You're gonna fucking murder them."

"It's not my call, Turk." The man paused. "Just go. Don't look back. This isn't on your conscience."

"Sir."

There was no response.

"Sir," Turk said again.

Still, no response.

He looked at the phone and saw that the call had been ended. He raised his arm, prepared to throw the phone, but decided against it. Instead, he crammed it into his pocket and walked past the grate on the floor. He lined the rifles along the wall, grabbed one, then walked back to the grate. The zombies on the floor beneath stared up at him. He looked past them and saw the seven men pressed against the back wall of a cell. He yelled out to them, and then began firing, picking off the afflicted beings below one at a time.

Three of the men in the cell began waving their arms, and Turk ceased fire.

"There's too many," one of them said.

"I don't care," Turk called back. "Can you open the cell?"

"No."

"Dammit." Turk lowered his weapon and wiped his brow. "Bombers are on the way. I gotta get this room cleared out."

"Oh shit," one of the men yelled. "They just broke through the main cell gate. They're gonna get to us soon."

Turk switched positions so he could see the entrance to the cell block. A line of zombies made their way through the outer hall within the cell block and stopped in front of the group of Deltas. They grabbed hold of the bars that line the cell and began shaking them. Turk knew that at some point the bars would give and crack at the joints. Turk took aim at the zombie at the head of the line. He started shooting. One by one, they went down until he had to stop to reload. That's when he heard the men shouting to get his attention.

"What?" Turk yelled.

The men yelled in unison, "Kill us!"

Turk shook his head in disbelief.

"Kill us," they repeated.

"Don't let them attack us, man," one called out. "You've seen what they do, right?"

Turk had seen what they could do. Ruiz's pain-filled eyes still haunted him. He saw them as if they were two feet in front of his face, dark and tortured.

"Kill us," the shouts continued, in unison, from below.

Turk scanned the area from all sides of the opening in the floor. There had to be a way to get them out. But the men were as far away from the stairwell door as they could be. There were hundreds of afflicted in between them and their escape, and now a horde of zombies lined up, a few feet from the men, like they were in line at a buffet. Soon enough, the doors to the restaurant would open, and the zombies would tear the men apart.

When his eyes fell back on the men, he saw that they'd turned their backs to him. They stood shoulder to shoulder, their arms wrapped around the backs of the men next to them. It wouldn't be murder, Turk told himself. They'd asked for it. Rather than die at the hands of the afflicted, they'd rather another soldier take them out. They wanted a clean death, a warrior's death, and Turk could give it to them. He had to. He'd want it for himself.

He dropped to one knee and took aim on the man in the middle. He took a second to ask God for forgiveness, and then he pulled the trigger. The bullet entered the man's skull from behind and his body slumped, but did not fall. The men on either side held him up. Turk paid no attention to the pink cloud that hovered in the air. Tears fell from his eyes as he selected another man at random. One by one, he laid the surviving men from Delta to rest, saving the men on the end for last.

After the last man fell, Turk stepped back, and then fell to his knees. He cursed himself for what he'd done and for what he'd have to do. Time was running out, and he had to escape before the bombers arrived.

He was about to rise to his feet when the door to the stairwell opened. Then, the buzzing that rose up through the grate was matched in intensity by the same sound, only from behind him.

Chapter 15

Sean found himself on his back, pinned down by the woman who had lunged at him from around the corner. Her blond hair hung down and fell across his face. The flap of skin that had peeled away from her head hovered inches away from his. He was drawn to her piercing blue eyes, which seemed brighter than they had through the window. He struggled against her grasp, but could not move. Her strength was far superior to his. Another effect of the mutation, he figured.

Why hadn't she tried to kill him yet? She remained on top of him, her head tilted to the side and her mouth closed.

What happened to Karl? Had she gotten to him first and Sean hadn't noticed?

She opened her mouth and a thick and phlegmy sound escaped. Small pieces of dirt fell from her lips and teeth and landed on Sean's cheek and between his parted lips. He started to spit them out, but stopped when her eyes narrowed in response. She continued to produce the sounds until she managed to form two words.

"Help... me."

Her voice was ragged and deep and gravelly.

"What can I do?" Sean said.

"Help me," she repeated.

"How?" Sean said through clenched teeth.

She let go of his shoulders and scooted back so that her legs straddled his waist. She settled onto his lap. Her eyes dimmed, then grew brighter, and he thought he saw a sliver of remaining humanity within them.

"How?" he asked again.

She licked her lips, to no apparent effect, then said, "Kill... Kill me... Kill me."

Sean lifted his torso and propped himself on his elbows. He began to scoot backward. She lifted up to allow him space to free himself. He reached down and felt for his pistol. His knuckles grazed along the inside of her bare thigh. Her skin felt like ice, and the experience sent a shiver up his arm.

He held the M9 in his right hand, cupping it with his left to keep it steady. He extended the gun. His shaky hands prevented him from holding his side arm level.

The woman leaned forward, resting her forehead against the end of the pistol's muzzle. She looked beyond the barrel, into his eyes, and smiled at him. Her eyes were brighter than Sean had ever seen them. She reached her hands out and placed them against the backs of Sean's, wrapping her fingers into his palms. Her touch was gentle, even if it was freezing. Her lips twitched and she managed to speak one last time.

"Thank you."

She closed her eyes.

Sean did the same as he pulled the trigger.

He felt her body fall to the side and heard it hit the floor with a slight thud. He reached down and lifted her left leg and pushed it off of his lap. He scooted away from her body, taking note of how at peace she looked. She was no longer the tortured beast who wandered the hallways seeking death. He wondered how long the soul could remain intact before being chased away. At what point did the human disappear, leaving only the zombie to inhabit the body?

"I thought for sure she was going to win."

Sean looked up and saw Karl seated against the wall across from him.

"I guess she did, in a way," Karl said.

"You sat there the whole time?" Sean stared at Karl in disbelief while shaking his head. "She could have killed me. Why didn't you do anything?"

Karl raised his arm, revealing a wide gash across his abdomen. His pants and the lower half of his shirt were soaked in blood. "She got me pretty good on her way to you. Don't know why. I'd have been happy to kill the bitch. Would have made much less of a production over it." He laughed, which caused his face to contort in pain.

Sean placed his pistol in his lap, then brought his hand to his cheeks, realizing too late that it was covered in the woman's blood. He used the sleeve of his left arm to wipe her remains from his face. He turned his head and gazed down the hall, past the control room, toward freedom. All he had to do was get up and start walking. If he encountered any zombies, he'd start firing. The important thing would be to keep moving. Besides, how many of them could there be on this level? He hadn't seen any patrolling the halls. They were either outside or on the floors below. The same place Turk and the rest of the SEAL team were.

Sean knew he couldn't leave. Not yet, at least. He had to find Turk.

Using the wall, Sean rose to his feet. "I'm going to look for Turk," he said to Karl. "You keep your eyes and ears open. If anyone but us approaches, you kill them. You got it, Karl?"

Karl nodded and whispered, "Yeah."

Sean thought about placing a bullet in Karl's head. After all, if Sean failed to locate Turk, Karl was as good as dead. Sean would be humane about killing the man. Those things wouldn't. In the end, he left the man alive. He started toward the corner and turned down the adjacent hallway.

Most of the lights were smashed out, leaving the hall dark and full of shadows. Shadows which seemed to dance around when Sean's eyes focused on another area. He wondered if the hall had been this dark when Turk and the others had come through, or had the woman or another zombie smashed all the lights out recently.

He tried not to think of what might be lurking in the darkened rooms he passed. His goal was to get to the next hallway then to the stairs. That's where he'd find Turk. He was sure of it. The stairs were the key to finding the remaining men and getting out of the building as a team.

These things we do so that others may live.

He picked up his pace as the light that flooded the hall from the adjacent corridor grew brighter. He had almost broken into a run when three afflicted beings stepped out from behind the wall, blocking his entrance to the corridor. Their eyes glowed bright, standing out amid their pale, shaded skin.

Sean stopped and reached for the MP7 strapped across his chest. He aimed and fired in a matter of seconds, sending three bullets flying, hitting one of the zombies in the face and forehead. It fell to the ground as the other two shuffled toward Sean.

Sean's initial panic began to fade. These weren't mutated in the same manner as those afflicted who could cross distances faster than any man. They were fifteen yards out and he felt as though he had plenty of time. He aimed at the one on the left, then squeezed the trigger. Three bullets launched in rapid succession. His aim had been off though, and the bullets started at dead center and then rose up into its neck. The wounds were fatal, not immediately so, though. Sean took a step back, re-aimed, fired. This time the first bullet slammed into the creature's forehead and the other two hit near enough.

The final zombie shuffled closer, now ten yards out.

Sean aimed and took a deep breath.

Eight yards out. Plenty of distance. Plenty of time.

Sean exhaled.

Seven yards, then six.

Sean pulled the trigger.

Nothing happened.

Five yards.

He squeezed the trigger, again.

Click. Nothing.

Four yards.

He let go of the MP7 and reached for his side arm. In his haste, he struggled to free the weapon from its holster.

Three yards, then two. With its outstretched arms, the zombie was no more than four feet away.

Sean freed his pistol and began firing wildly, hitting the afflicted being in its legs, then its torso and neck and head. It dropped to its knees, then fell forward, landing less than twelve inches from Sean's feet.

Sean bent over at the waist and dropped his face into his palms, searing his forehead against the scorching hot barrel of his M9. The pain of the burn helped him to focus. He steadied himself and placed his hands on his knees and took several deep breaths. He became aware of the fact that he did not have enough ammunition to continue. He'd have to double back and retrieve extra rounds from Karl, and maybe even get his M4 from the command room. Was there time, though? Sean straightened his body and turned at the waist to look down the dark corridor behind him.

His eyes were off the lifeless body in front of him for a few seconds, but that was all it took. In a flash, the zombie propelled itself up and forward, sinking its teeth into Sean's left leg, right above the knee.

Chapter 16

Turk stayed low and moved into the shadows along the edge of the room. The moment his back touched the wall, he flattened himself against it. Five dark figures and five sets of bright eyes passed through the open doorway. They entered in a single file line, shuffling tight to one another. The one at the front of the line scanned the room, his eyes moving from the right to the left. His gaze passed by Turk, then stopped a second later. Those glowing eyes scanned the area around Turk, taking their time, but never stopping on him. The zombie's head swung to the right and it began shuffling along the outer perimeter of the room, toward the wall opposite Turk's position.

Turk lifted his foot, began sidestepping to his right, toward the doorway. If he could avoid having to discharge his weapon, he would. It would only take one of those damn *things* to reach him for it to all be over. There was no one else alive, which meant there was no one who could save him if he were attacked. Turk was no longer on the offensive. The name of the game had become survival.

He caught a glimpse of the remains of Ruiz and the other men. So many lives lost, and for no good reason. They should have been told what they were getting into instead of being fed a bullshit story. The anger rose inside of him like the bitter taste of bile in his throat. How could he face the families of the men who'd lost their lives under his command?

Turk noticed that the pain in his arm had intensified and traveled from his forearm to his shoulder. What if he had become infected from the bite? Screw it, he thought. Let him become infected. Then those in command would pay. Turk'd be their worst nightmare if he became a zombie.

From that point on, Turk alternated between looking at the door to the stairs, and the creatures on the wall opposite him. They didn't seem to notice that he was in the room. Or perhaps they didn't care. Whatever the reason, he decided not to wait around and find out. He knew there could be more of them waiting for him once he stepped into the stairwell. However, he'd deal with that if and when it was necessary.

As he approached the remaining bodies of his team, Turk stopped. He contemplated gathering something from each man to return to their families. He decided against it, though, realizing that anything they wore might contain traces of whatever it was that turned humans into the creatures that rattled the bowels of the facility. The thought crossed his mind again that he might be infected. And at that moment, he realized that he'd been feeling lightheaded and nauseous since he'd been bitten. He wondered if the sickness could be transferred through bodily fluids.

It didn't matter. Turk had decided he wouldn't die inside the facility. He'd rather stand on solid ground and let a five-hundred pound bomb finish him off while the sun shone on his ass, than to go down amid the foul stench that surrounded him.

He looked away from the room where the bodies of tortured souls and the bodies of his fellow SEALs lay. Turk stepped through the doorway, pulling it shut tight behind him, sealing off the stairwell. He clutched the MP7 in both hands, inched to his right to check the stairs that led down to the third floor. They were empty, save for the smeared blood that covered each step. Satisfied that there was no immediate threat, he started up the stairs.

As Turk approached the landing, he heard a scream from further up the stairwell. The scream was not one of the afflicted, though. It belonged to a human. He knew at that moment someone was still alive. Turk ran up the stairs, ignoring the pain in his arm that flared up with each jarring step.

He rounded the corner to the final set of stairs and froze in his tracks. At the top, on the landing stood one of them. It hunched over and stared down at him with menacing red eyes.

Turk attempted to aim, but before he could set his sights, the zombie leapt from the platform. Turk fired without aiming, spraying the air with three burst shots. The zombie's body flinched a few times, and Turk figured he landed a couple shots, but had no idea where. Not the head, he guessed by the way the creature began clawing at his face after it landed on top of him.

Turk's weapon had been knocked loose from his hands and he was unable to regain control of it. He reached up and grabbed the afflicted by its neck, holding his arms at full extension to keep the zombie's mouth as far away as possible. Thick strands of saliva dripped from its mouth and onto Turk's wrists and forearms. No matter how hard Turk squeezed, the zombie didn't seem to notice. It kept snapping away at the air, perhaps expecting that Turk's face would be within range at some point.

Turk let go with his right hand and let his arm fall. He rolled onto his left side and drew his right knee up, allowing him to reach the knife he had sheathed against his calf. The blade slipped out of its leather holster. Turk brought the knife up, adjusting it so that the blade faced the hostile being on top of him. With a quick and decisive movement, Turk whipped his arm toward his head, then swung it toward the zombie, driving the knife through its left eye, into its brain. The zombie went limp. Turk shoved it to the left, pushing and kicking to get the foul creature off of his body.

Turk rose and fired three rounds into the zombie's head, ensuring it had experienced an unpleasant second death.

He raced to the top of the stairs and stopped at the foot of the hallway. The screams were louder here, and he now knew for sure they belonged to a human. Turk ran down the corridor, turned left at the adjoining hall and raced to the end where it met with the main perimeter hallway. He peeked around the corner and saw a body on the floor, then another, and beyond that, two bodies that seemed to be joined together. He shone his light and saw that an afflicted was on top of Sean, and the PJ seemed to be losing the battle.

Turk squeezed the trigger of his MP7, firing the rounds into the ceiling in an effort to distract the zombie. It worked. The being rose up from Sean's body and faced Turk.

Turk shone his light and saw the being's face covered in blood. Turk's heart sunk as he feared for Sean's life. Without hesitation, he fired, hitting the zombie in the chest. He lined up his next shot and sent three bullets flying. The first shot was true, and the zombie fell.

Turk stepped over the dead being and knelt next to Sean. "Ryder," Turk said. "Talk to me."

"My leg," Ryder said.

Turk looked down and saw that Ryder's leg had been chewed to the bone, perhaps into it, right above the knee. He feared that the femoral artery had been severed and that Ryder would bleed out. There was already a significant puddle of blood on the floor.

"Sean," Turk said. "Listen to me. I'm going to apply a tourniquet to your leg. Okay? You understand?"

Ryder opened his eyes and nodded, then he said, "What happened to your arm?"

"One of them bit me, too."

Ryder reached into his pocket and pulled out the syringe.

"What's that?" Turk said.

"Antidote," Ryder said. "Should be three doses. One for you, one for me, and one for Karl, if it's not too late."

Turk tried not to show any excitement over the fact that one of his men was still alive. He finished applying the tourniquet to Ryder's leg, then he grabbed the syringe and pulled the cap off. He stuck the needle into Sean's right thigh, and pressed the plunger, dispensing about a third of the liquid into the PJ. He pulled the syringe out, wiped it on a clean patch of his shirt, then stuck it in his own arm, being careful to use only half of the remaining liquid. He pulled it back out and capped it, then stuck it in his pocket.

"I don't think I can walk," Ryder said, offering a half-smile.

Turk figured most men displayed some kind of false bravado in situations like this. He was certain that Ryder had seen it time and again during his missions and now was giving Turk the same treatment.

"Don't worry," Turk said. "I got you. Just tell me if something comes at us from behind."

"I'll do better," Ryder said. "I'll shoot the bastards."

"Make sure you give me a warning," Turk said as he lifted Ryder off the ground and placed him over his shoulder. "I'd rather not go deaf in here."

Both men looked at each other and laughed.

Turk hustled down the hall, and then slowed as he approached the corner. There was no stealthy way to check around the corner without setting Sean down, and Turk didn't want to do that, as it might place the man at risk of going into shock. Turk stepped around with his weapon aimed in front of him. He saw Karl sitting on the floor, leaning back against the wall. Karl's eyes were closed and his head bent over. Turk couldn't tell if the man was dead or not.

"Karl," Turk said.

Karl said nothing, didn't move.

Turk stayed close to the opposite wall as he passed in front of Karl. He decided to address the man one more time.

"Karl? You okay?"

This time Karl nodded and opened his eyes. The glow they gave off was bright and intense. Turk also noticed how pale the man's skin had become.

"Ryder, you think this antidote works if they've turned already?"

"No," Sean said. "The doctor said that would be too late."

"What doctor?"

"The doctor in the control room—"

"Never mind," Turk said. "You tell me later. Okay, Sean? For now, watch your ears."

Turk lifted his gun and aimed it at Karl, or rather, the being that had once been Karl. He had to think of him in those terms in order to do what had to be done. With a deep breath and a heavy heart, Turk sent three bullets into his old teammate, then turned and began running down the hall. He had no idea how long it had been since he spoke with his CO. He only knew that time was running out and it wouldn't be long before the bombs began to fall.

Chapter 17

The final fifty feet might as well have been a mile. Lactic acid had built up in Turk's muscles and his legs burned. It took every bit of willpower he had to keep his knees pumping as he sprinted toward the tunnel that would lead them out of the facility. Getting Sean to this point had been easy, relatively speaking. Now he had to figure out how to get him to the surface while traveling through a space where neither of the men could stand up straight. He looked at Sean and performed a quick assessment of the PJ. He looked awful. He looked like a dead man. Turk wondered if Sean would be able to save a man in his condition. The thought of leaving Sean there to ensure his own safe escape crossed Turk's mind. But he couldn't do that. He'd already left so many behind, and adding one more would break him.

"You with me, Sean?" Turk said.

"Yeah," Sean said through gritted teeth.

"I'm gonna need you to do some of the work here. Okay?" He set Ryder down inside the bottom lip of the tunnel. "Can you drag yourself up?"

Sean strained and grunted and pushed himself onto his right knee. Then, with Turk's help, he stood on his right foot, letting his left leg trail behind. He shuffled around and screamed. However, the pain did not stop the man. He kept moving forward.

Turk climbed through the narrow opening, then rose to his feet in a hunched over position. He wrapped his left arm around Ryder, providing the man with extra support. He intended to help take some pressure off Ryder's decimated leg. The two men huddled together and began making their way up the angled tunnel. After twenty feet, the buzzing that had remained constant during their stay in the facility, faded away.

"Watch for zombies," Ryder said.

Turk smiled for a second or two when he realized that Sean had been calling the afflicted beings zombies as well. The moment of revelation passed, and he resumed feeling as though they were being followed by a horde of the creatures. Every fifteen seconds or so, he'd check over his shoulder to verify the tunnel was clear. He saw nothing each time he looked back. However, the feeling that the zombies were close by helped push Turk forward when all he wanted to do was collapse.

Turk thought back to when they entered the facility. How long had it taken them to travel through the tunnel? Was it three minutes? Five? Ten? How could something so recent feel like it had taken place so long ago? Why couldn't he remember a detail like that? However long it had taken, he was sure that the journey out was going to take three times as long with the injured man slowing him down. Once again, the thought of leaving Ryder behind crossed Turk's mind. But when he looked over at Sean and saw the determination on the man's pale face, he knew he had to keep pushing on with him. Then Sean went limp and nearly dragged both Turk and himself to the ground.

"Get up, Sean," Turk said.

"I can't do this, Turk," Ryder said. "Too much blood loss. Leave me."

"Dammit, Ryder, if you'd pulled this twenty seconds ago I'd have left your ass. But you're on my conscience now. You got that?"

Sean said nothing. His eyes fluttered back in his head.

"Get up, Sean," Turk said. "Come on. Stand up, then take one step, then another. You can do this. I want you to think about how, in a couple weeks, you and I are gonna hook up and have some drinks and all of this will be a memory. We'll laugh about it as we pound back a case."

Ryder released a primal scream as he pushed himself off the ground. It was a yell Turk was familiar with, having heard it weekly since his days in BUDs training. He helped Sean balance on his good leg, and then they resumed moving through the tunnel.

"Let's see if we can pick it up," Turk said. "I don't know how much longer we have."

"Till what?"

"They're bombing this place."

Turk assumed his words motivated Ryder, because the man began moving twice as fast, jumping forward with his good leg, screaming in pain when his left foot slammed into the ground. But to Turk, every cry meant they were closer to leaving the nightmare behind. They might make it out, after all.

The closer they got to the end of the tunnel, the wider it became, and it soon became possible for Turk to carry Ryder. It couldn't have come at a better time, too. Sean's head and torso were soaked in sweat, and his left leg covered in blood. Turk became concerned that the tourniquet had slipped. That would guarantee death for the PJ. If it had, there was nothing Turk could do, so he cast his doubts aside and pressed on.

"Stay with me, Sean."

"I'm right here, Turk."

They reached the end of the tunnel, and Turk fell to his knees, mostly in thanks, but partially due to exhaustion. But he knew the journey was not yet complete. They had to get out and they had to get away from the site before the bombs started falling from the sky. Turk eased Ryder to the ground, then got back on his feet. He stepped toward the door, placed his hand on the knob and spun it to the left until he heard a click.

"I'm gonna check it out first," Turk said.

Ryder nodded and said nothing as he glanced down toward his leg. Turk noticed a bemused look wash over Sean's face.

"What?" Turk said.

"I'm gonna lose my leg."

"I know. I'm sorry, man."

"Why did my last jump have to be at night?"

Turk forced a smile and placed his hand on Sean's shoulder, giving it a reassuring squeeze. Then he cracked the door and bright sunlight flooded the tunnel, setting his eyes on fire and killing his vision. He blinked a few times and shielded his eyes from the sun while they adjusted to the light. He almost wished they hadn't, because the sight before him gave him little hope for them escaping alive. He pushed the door shut, turned around and leaned back against it. He brought his palms to his face and rubbed his stubbled head.

"Think you can still shoot?" Turk asked.

"I can probably manage," Sean said, using the wall to help him stand up.

"Here." Turk handed Sean his MP7. "Anything approaches, squeeze the trigger." He handed him an extra magazine before turning back toward the door. "I don't care what it looks like, Sean. Kill it."

He half expected the fifty or so zombies he saw outside to rush toward the tunnel when he pushed the door open again. But they didn't. They didn't even seem to care that he and Sean were in the doorway. They all stood with their backs to the men, facing the rising sun. Their bodies were arched, their arms wide, and their faces turned up toward the sky. Turk wondered if the action was some sort of spiritual cleansing for the damned.

He took note of their positions, then he raised his rifle and aimed at the closest zombie.

"Don't," Ryder said.

"What?"

"Wait."

"Why?"

"Help me through the door." Ryder held out his right arm.

Turk reached over to support Sean as he limped through the doorway. "What are we doing, Ryder?"

"Listen."

Turk angled his head, but didn't hear anything. He shrugged and shook his head as he looked back at Sean.

"We need to move away from the door," Sean said.

"That's going to put us out in the open, closer to them."

"I know," Sean said. "Just do it."

Turk wrapped his left arm around Sean and helped him move away from the facility's entrance. They traveled ten feet, then Sean said, "Hear it?"

Turk squinted and angled his head while scanning the crowd of zombies who were still distracted by the morning sun and blue sky. Or were they in awe of it?

As if he had read Turk's thoughts, Sean said, "It's not the sun. It's the planes. They hear and feel them."

Planes. Bombers.

"Sean, we gotta get moving. Fast. Those are the bombers, and they're headed straight for us."

"The sound must resonate with them. Soothe their soul, so to speak," Ryder said.

"I don't care," Turk said. "As long as they don't care about us."

They moved away from the crowd of the afflicted that gathered between the entrance and the makeshift graveyard. Not a single one of them looked back at the two men.

"They don't even know we're here," Turk said.

"Maybe it's too bright," Sean said. "No shadows. I think they respond to our—"

"Whatever. We're making a break for it." Turk hoisted Sean up to a fireman's carry and began to head for the hill. The planes were close. He tossed a glance over his shoulder to see if he had visible contact with them yet. There was still no sign of them, other than the sound of their approach. Turk's eyes scanned the group of zombies one last time, then shifted to the graveyard. What he saw made him pause. "Jesus Christ. Sean, look."

"What?" Ryder said.

"The graveyard."

"Jesus."

A hand stuck out from the dirt, its fingers pointing straight up. Then an arm pushed through, even further out of the ground, almost to the shoulder. Another hand emerged, followed by the top of a head, then eyes and a nose and, finally, a complete face. The same thing happened at a second grave, and then a third. Within seconds, half the dirt mounds had bodies pushing up through the disturbed earth. Perhaps the phrase zombies had been more accurate than Turk had realized.

"Move," Sean said.

Turk pushed harder and faster with every step, reaching the top of the hill in less time than they had taken to descend it the night before. They went over the ridge, and he set Sean down and reached for his satellite and cellular telephones. He turned to hand one to Sean, but the man had passed out. Turk pushed down a single number on each phone and waited for the first person to pick up. His CO answered. Turk explained that he and Ryder were out, but that Sean needed medical attention as soon as possible or he'd die. His CO told him to leave his satellite phone on. They had a team close by who would locate them through the phone's GPS chip, which acted like a beacon and provided Turk's location in case of an emergency. Then, he told him to get moving, because the bombers were only minutes away.

Turk lifted Sean over his shoulder, picked a line, and started running. He sprinted faster and harder and longer than he ever had in his life. He didn't dare stop. He didn't have to look over his shoulder to know that the bombers had arrived. The first explosion gave that away.

Turk yelled as each subsequent bomb screeched through the air and pummeled the ground with devastating impact. He felt the earth shake and ripple under his feet. How close would the bombs get to their position? Did the pilots know that two U.S. soldiers were on the ground? Would they make it out of this alive?

All the pain Turk felt, his burning lungs and aching legs and cramping muscles, none of it made a difference after the bomb landed too close to him and Sean. The initial impact did not affect them, but the subsequent blast wave did. The sudden burst of hot air traveling at over one hundred miles per hour knocked Turk off his feet, sending him through the air and jarring Sean loose from his grip.

Turk landed violently, first on the back of his head, then his spine. He bounced a few feet in the air and his body twisted and he was slammed onto his side. He skid five or ten feet before coming to a stop face down in the dirt. The last thing he saw before passing out was Sean's bloody leg landing five feet in front of him, sending a cloud of dust two feet into the air.

Chapter 18

"Stay with us, Ryder."

Sean opened his eyes and saw two faces hovering over him. He figured out he was inside a helicopter by the thumping of the rotors and the whine of the turbine. But why was he there, lying on his back?

"We're gonna take care of you." He couldn't tell which of them said it. Their faces were dark and indistinguishable and contrasted sharply with the bright light behind their heads.

Sean barely heard the words, although he could tell the man was no more than eighteen inches away. If not for the constant thumping and whining created by the helicopter, he would have been concerned that he'd lost his hearing. He tried to turn his head to the left, but found himself unable to do so. Then he tried to lift his head, but couldn't. He'd been immobilized. His training had taught him there was one reason for that. He broke into a cold sweat. They were concerned about his neck. Why, though? Had he broken it? Had he not managed to deploy his reserve chute after his main failed to launch, and somehow he'd survived the impact, but had broken his neck?

Sean searched his mind in an effort to recall the last thing he saw before waking up in the chopper.

The sun blinded him. It exploded in front of him. But, was it the sun? He had been outside and there was a flash of light. His body was launched through the air ten or fifteen or twenty feet. He flew, his body twisting, turning, slamming into the ground. He landed on his back with tremendous force. Had he shattered his spine? No, that much he knew. He recalled moving, if only a bit, in an effort to check on Turk.

Turk!

What had happened to the SEAL?

"T-T-Turk," Sean said.

"Save your strength, Sergeant," one of the men said.

"Where's Turk?"

Neither man replied. They looked at one another without giving Sean's question the attention it deserved. He asked several more times. They continued to ignore him. He decided to wait before asking again. Someone had to know and that person would tell him. Until then, he had to focus on remaining awake so that he could stay alive. Sleep could mean shock. And, judging by the pain in his left leg, shock would mean death if the wound was as bad as he thought it was.

"Cold," Sean said.

"You've lost a lot of blood," the man said. "I've started a transfusion."

Combat doc, Sean thought. He didn't recognize the man, but his thoughts were jumbled and he didn't know if the two had worked together before or not.

"I'm going to level with you, Ryder," the man said. "I don't know if we're going to be able to save your leg. But it was heads up on your part applying the tourniquet to it. Saved your life, man. When you're better, you'll have to tell me how you managed to do that after stepping on an IED."

There was too much recognition in the way the man spoke to him. How did this man know Sean? He was certain he had never seen him before. What was he talking about, stepping on an IED? He'd been hit by a bomb. A bomb dropped by a U.S. plane. It wasn't the bomb that took his leg, it was a damn zombie.

"Zombie," Sean said.

The men looked down at him, their faces disappearing again as their heads blocked out the light.

"What?" one of them said.

"No IED," Sean said. "And it was Turk who saved me. I didn't have," he paused and forced himself to swallow, "I had no strength."

The men looked up and nodded at each other. One twisted at the waist and returned with a needle. He stuck it in Sean's shoulder and pressed on the plunger.

Sean felt fire blaze through his arm as the fluid coursed through his veins. Inch by inch, his body went numb, starting with his arm, then spreading across his chest and down his abdomen. The heat turned to cold, traveled up his neck, surrounded his head. His eyelids grew heavier with every blink he took as the agent penetrated his brain. Finally, his eyes shut and remained closed. The thumping of the rotor and the whine of the turbine were drowned out, and Sean went to sleep.

The quiet and still surprised Sean when he woke up. Had the shock and blood loss been too much? Was he dead? He tried to move his head and his hands and his feet. Pain flooded his body, confirming that he had not died. One nightmare had ended, and another one had begun. The nerves in his left leg were on fire, at least to a spot above his knee. Below that, he felt nothing. His lungs and chest ached with every breath he took, leading him to believe that he had multiple broken ribs. His head was no longer restrained, and he shook it slowly side-to-side. He tried to speak, but was unable to.

"Doctor," a female voice said with a Nigerian accent. "He's moving."

"Christ," a man with the same accent said. "Someone get the anesthetist in here. I thought they took care of this on the way here."

Sean forced his heavy eyelids open. He was greeted by a bright halo of light that washed out his vision. He made out shapes along his left and right, but could not see where he was.

"Sir," the man said. "My name is Doctor Adebayo. I'm sorry to have to tell you this, but we are in the process of amputating your leg. The men that brought you here explained to me that you are a highly trained medical technician in the United States Air Force. So what I'm about to tell you should make sense. We thought you were anesthetized prior to being delivered to us."

A memory struck Sean and he recalled one of the men in the helicopter injecting something into his arm. He'd passed out right afterward and, as far as he could tell, had been under until he woke up here. Perhaps the antidote that Turk had injected him with while they were still inside the facility had something to do with the anesthesia not working properly? He opened his mouth to say something to that effect, but the doctor continued.

"For some reason, you've come out of it. I've already removed the tourniquet and prepped your leg for amputation. I have to proceed at once, or we run the risk of your blood pressure elevating too high and remaining there, leading to you bleeding out or having a stroke on the table. If I don't begin now, you will die. Do you understand what I'm telling you?"

Sean took a moment to process the doctor's words. His leg was gone. He knew that before he escaped from the halls of that underground hell, where he thought he was going to die. He'd felt okay when he believed he'd end up dead. In some ways, he almost preferred to die rather than live his life with one leg. If not for the memories of his wife Kathy and daughter Emma, he might have struggled against the team of medical staff that surrounded him. But he had to leave alive. He had to be there for his family.

Warm tears flooded his eyes and fell down the sides of his face in a constant stream. A heavy leather strap was placed over his waist and cinched down, drawing him tight to the bed. Fingers brushed up against his palms and wrapped around his wrist. Hands pressed down against his shoulders, pinning him down. A woman leaned over him, blocking out the bright light that now silhouetted her. She forced a smile, but his pain was reflected in her eyes. Or was it pity that she showed him? She used one hand to pinch his face near the corners of his jaw, forcing his mouth open. She maintained her grip, then, with her free hand, inserted what Sean assumed was a bite stick.

They were going to begin the amputation without anesthesia.

"This is going to hurt worse than anything you've ever felt," the doctor said.

If he could have spoken, Sean would have offered an argument to the man. As far as he was concerned, nothing could be more painful than placing the barrel of your gun against your best friend's head and pulling the trigger. And, perhaps, this was Sean's penance for doing so.

The doctor continued. "We'll have you under anesthesia as soon as possible, but I cannot wait any longer to begin."

He started the bone saw, an oscillating saw equipped with a diamond tipped blade, emitting a high pitched *whirr*. Sean didn't lift his head, but he imagined that the saw was one of the larger models. He knew that hundreds of years ago amputations had been performed on the battlefield using manual saws. This thought left him feeling fortunate that his procedure would be over in a matter of a few minutes.

The doctor slipped out of the lower range of Sean's field of vision. Sean prepared himself for what was to come. He bit down on the rod between his teeth and squeezed the hands next to his at his side. He saw a pained look flash across one man's face. Then he saw disgust across the other man's face. The woman behind him stroked his hair with one hand as she held the straps affixed to each end of the bite stick with her other hand, keeping the rod firmly in place between Sean's teeth.

The diamond tipped blade met Sean's femur with a sickening screech. His body tried to jolt upward, but the leather belt and strong hands and arms kept him rooted to the operating table. His gargled screams drowned out the sound of the bone saw as it tore through the few remaining scraps of meat, muscle and tendons covering his femur.

The saw worked in a single constant action, and the doctor maintained enough pressure to drive it downward, severing the thick bone in two.

The woman behind him and the man to his left separated, and an older woman appeared in between them. Her ashen, wrinkled skin told Sean that she'd been in the hospital for a number of years, and had probably seen worse injuries than his. But the look on her face told him that she'd never seen a man being put through an amputation while awake and aware. She spoke, but Sean didn't listen. If he could have talked at that moment, he would have told her that she was too late, but she was welcome to stick around for a bit. Mercifully, she inserted a needle into his neck, presumably to speed up the process of the anesthesia shutting off the nerve center in his brain from the rest of his body.

The halo of light closed in above Sean. The dark faces shrunk and disappeared as the outer edges of his vision turned gray, then black. Starting with his hands and feet, his body became numb. A welcome relief as the sensation traveled through his legs. A moment before he lost all sensation, he thought that he felt a tiny prick in his left thigh. He wondered if she had injected another agent into his leg. Although, it could have been the bone saw.

The light faded out, as did the voices and sounds in the room. Sean entered a blackened space, where tall grasses swayed in a gentle breeze, brushing against his palm as he walked toward the images of his wife and daughter.

Chapter 19

A week passed by in less than ten minutes for Sean. They kept him sedated for the most part, an effort to help with the initial healing of the amputated limb. If he was asleep, he wouldn't move. It also meant fewer pain medications, allowing his body to work as it needed to in order to heal the wound in as short a time as possible. His time awake was filled with doctors and nurses, an ambulance, and a plane.

He woke up in considerable pain and with no idea where he was. The room was quite different to the one he recalled being in the day before. He glanced to his right where a sliver of light sneaked into the room through an opening between heavy gray drapes. It took him a moment to realize that it was snowing outside. He knew he wasn't in southern Nigeria anymore. Had they transported him across the Atlantic? Was he in Walter Reed?

He looked to his left. Tears flooded his eyes at the two beautiful faces staring back at him. Through most of the ordeal inside the facility, Sean had been able to suppress his thoughts and feelings about his wife and daughter. Sean had always figured that thinking too much of his loved ones was a sure fire way to get himself killed. That's why he'd always kissed the picture of them before the start of a mission, and tucking the photo away put them out of his mind, at least until it was safe enough for him to think about them again.

"Kathy," Sean said. "Emma."

His wife stood and picked up their daughter, leaning her over Sean to give him a hug. Sean reached up with both arms, wrapping one around Emma, and the other around Kathy. For the first time in more than a week, he felt at peace. Then, he began to cry. He wept for Jules, and the SEAL team, and the tortured souls that were forever trapped in that underground lair of death.

Sean released his wife and child. Kathy set Emma on the chair and handed the little girl a coloring book. Then she turned back to Sean.

"I heard about Jules," she said.

Sean bit his lip and nodded. He wondered how much she knew and what he should tell her. Hell, what *could* he tell her? Truth was, he wasn't sure what had happened anymore. His dreams had been full of so many vivid and horrific events, the lines between reality and fantasy had become blurred.

Kathy saved him from having to make the decision. "Let's talk about that later, Sean," she said, gripping his shoulder and squeezing gently.

Sean brought his palms to his face and wiped away his tears, feeling for the first time the growth of hair on his cheeks. He nodded at Kathy, and then looked at the equipment above him. It was then that he realized he was not at Walter Reed. The equipment labels were written in another language and he realized he was in Europe.

"Where are we?" he asked.

"Germany," Kathy replied.

He thought for a minute. There were several U.S. Air Force bases in Germany. He figured they would have taken him to the largest.

"Frankfurt?" he said.

"No," she said. "Near Munich."

"Erding?" he said, referring to the Air Force base about half an hour north of Munich.

"No, it's a private place, Sean. You are here to see Doctor Kaufmann."

"Who's that?"

She shrugged. The gesture led Sean to believe she'd only remained a little more informed than himself. "He's a leader in prosthetics. They used the word *pioneer*. That's all I know. The Air Force set all this up. They promised me they're going to take care of you." She hesitated, then added, "Take care of us."

"How's that?"

"They'll be in to talk to you. They asked me to let them tell you."

Sean shrugged, then slid his hand under the sheets toward his left thigh. He felt the bandaged stump that signified where his leg had been severed. He scratched at the bandages that covered the closed wound around his femur. He wanted to pull back the sheets and inspect it, but didn't out of fear of frightening his wife and daughter.

"How's it feel?" Kathy asked.

"Hurts," Sean replied. "Are you going to be okay with this?" he added.

She lifted her shoulders and inch and forced a smile. "I'll be there for you no matter what, Babe."

Sean hoped she'd meant it, because he knew he'd need her now more than ever. Recovering from the wound was one thing. Recovering mentally from the things he had encountered in Nigeria was another. He knew that at some point he'd need to tell someone, and he knew that someone would likely be her. He was concerned that the things he had to tell her might be enough to make her run away from him.

"It's close to Emma's nap time," Kathy said. "We've been here all morning waiting for you to wake up."

"Sorry it took so long," Sean said with a smile.

"You snore, Daddy," Emma said without looking up from her coloring book.

Sean laughed, perhaps for the first time since Jules had been attacked that night in Nigeria.

"We're staying across the street," Kathy said. "They put us up in an apartment there. We have it for a month, although they told us they doubt we'll be here that long."

"Okay," Sean said, deciding not to ask who *they* were.

"We'll be back around eight in the morning to join you for breakfast."

He didn't want them to leave, but he also knew that it had to be tough for Emma to see her daddy laid up in bed, unable to move. He had no idea what his face looked like, if it were covered in cuts, scrapes and bruises. He wasn't sure if his daughter knew that his leg had been taken. If she did, then he figured the question on her mind was "how" and sooner or later she'd ask. He knew that he wasn't comfortable enough to answer that question.

"Okay," he managed, forcing a smile to linger on his face until his wife and daughter had left the room and were out of sight. A wave of calm washed over him. Despite all that had happened and everything he'd lost physically, mentally and spiritually, he still had his family. He knew that there were soldiers he served alongside whose families no longer had them.

He realized that he hadn't had solid food since before he entered the facility in Nigeria with Jules, Turk and the rest of SEAL Team 8. His stomach turned and ached at the thought of eating, and he hoped that the hospital would provide him with an early dinner.

It took an hour and a half before a nurse came by with his meal. The food they provided held little appeal for Sean, but he ate it anyway. He needed strength and now was as good a time as any to begin rebuilding it. Before he finished with his meal, there was a knock on his door. He had been expecting the doctor, so receiving a visitor at the late hour was of little surprise.

However, the four men who entered his room were unexpected.

Chapter 20

The first man through the door was tall and lean. He appeared to be around fifty. His receding hair was half-black, half-gray, and he was dressed casually. In fact, they all were. The other men were young, though. They looked to be around the same age as Sean. He didn't recognize any of them, but figured them to be military, or worse, CIA. The facility in Nigeria was the kind of place the Agency would know about and want to keep tabs on. That would explain why they'd come to see Sean. They wanted to extract whatever information he had.

"Staff Sergeant Ryder?" the older man said.

Sean stared at the man, but did not reply.

"Are you Staff Sergeant Sean Ryder?" the man asked again.

"Yeah," Sean replied. "Who're you?"

The man turned toward the others, and then motioned with his hand. One guy left the room, pulling the door closed behind him. The remaining two men stood by the door, one on either side with their hands crossed in front of their waists. Sean noticed the tell-tale bulge on their right hips, indicating they were armed. And, he presumed, dangerous.

"Who are you?" Sean asked again.

"My name is Kemp," the man said. "That's all you need to know. These other men are here to make sure you and I are left alone while we talk."

"That's funny," Sean said. "I would've assumed they were here to make sure that I talked."

Kemp nodded and offered a curt smile. "I understand your apprehension, Sean. You've been through a lot these last few days. I'm here to help, not hurt. Work with me and everything will be taken care of for you. Understand?"

"Who do you work for? Are you with the Air Force? The Navy?"

Kemp smiled, and said, "That's not important, Sean. What is important is that we discuss what happened in Nigeria."

Sean felt his skin flush and a thin layer of sweat formed on his brow. "What do you know about it?"

"You went there on a support mission," Kemp said. "The Army lost a company of Rangers, and a handful of operatives from Delta Force."

Sean nodded.

"You and your partner, Staff Sergeant Julian Hoover, were set to rendezvous with members of SEAL Team 8. But the last contact from them stated that you and Hoover never arrived. They figured that you two were—"

"Wait," Sean said. "What?"

"They figured you two were blown off course," Kemp continued, seemingly annoyed by Sean's interruption. "They backtracked to where they estimated you should have landed, but there was no sign of either of you."

"I don't know what you're talking about. We were a little behind them, but not by much. It took us maybe a half-hour to reach them."

Kemp furrowed his brow and tilted his head to the side. "No, Sean, you never reached them. You don't remember what happened after you landed?"

"Of course I do," Sean said. "How could I forget it? We encountered..." Sean paused, trying to think of a word other than zombie. "A humanoid being attacked Jules and me. We killed it. Then we hustled and found Turk and the rest of—"

"You stepped on an IED, Sean. We determined the spot where you landed, which was damn close to a terrorist training camp by the way. From there, you set off to the south, but you didn't make it a quarter-mile before you stepped on the explosive."

Sean shook his head furiously. "That's not what happened."

"Are you sure?" Kemp leaned in close to Sean and gestured toward his shortened left leg. "You were the lucky one here. Hoover took shrapnel to the head and died instantly."

Sean continued to shake his head. "That's not true. We met up with the SEALs. Ask Turk. As far as I know he's still a—"

"Who is Turk? By my count, you've mentioned him twice now. I've never heard that name before."

"Charles Turksen," Sean said. "He led the SEAL team."

Kemp's lower lip protruded, he shrugged. "I don't know of a SEAL by that name, Sean." He pulled out his cell phone and flipped it open. He stuck his fingertip on the number pad and held a button down for a few seconds, and then he lifted the phone to his head. After a moment, he said, "Yeah, this is Kemp. Tell me, do you have any information on a Charles Turksen, USN, SEAL, maybe goes by Turk?" Kemp looked at Sean and faked a smile. "Yeah, I'm here with him now. He states that they rendezvoused with the SEAL team, and met with this Turksen. Says he was in charge." Another pause. "Okay, yeah, sounds good. I'll be waiting for your call."

Sean waited while the man folded his phone and placed it in his back pocket.

"They're going to dig a little deeper," Kemp said. "But his initial search had no records of any Turk or Turksen."

Sean started to rattle off the names of the other men who had perished.

Kemp nodded. "Yes, those men are dead, Sean. They were ambushed almost immediately after they set up camp for the night.

Had you not stepped on that explosive, they would have killed you as well. Although, some might argue that they were alerted to the SEAL team's presence when you stepped on the IED."

"I don't know who you are," Sean said. "But you need to listen to me. I didn't step on any damn explosive. Those men weren't ambushed after they landed. We stayed on the ground for almost twenty-four hours, and then we entered a facility. They were doing biological testing down there and there were," Sean looked at the men behind Kemp, then lowered his voice, "mutated humans in there. Vicious, mindless killers. Those *things*, zombies we called them, they killed the men. One of them attacked my leg. That's how I lost it. It wasn't a damn IED."

Kemp frowned as he tilted his head. He looked at Sean with soft eyes, perhaps pitying him. "Are you sure that really happened, Sean? I mean, do you hear yourself? Zombies?" He laughed.

"Yes, I know exactly what happened, and I know what I saw in that hell hole."

"You've been unconscious for more than a week, and under quite a heavy sedative. The stuff they gave you has been known to help a man to reach into the deepest recesses of his imagination, and pull out of it some pretty dark and crazy things. Disturbing dreams are most often reported. So are hallucinations. I've read stories much like the one you recounted, although aliens or demons are the most common vision. In fact—" Kemp's ringing phone interrupted him. "I'm sorry. Let me grab this."

Kemp backed away from the bed and answered his phone. "Didn't find any record of him, eh? I didn't think you would. That's the kind of name I'd remember."

Sean leaned back until his pillow enveloped him. What was going on? None of it made sense. His mind swam in doubt as he tried to recall what had really happened in Nigeria. His own vision seemed so real and accurate. However, he could picture Kemp's version with clarity. Logically, which made more sense? That he'd lost his leg due to a zombie bite, or an explosive? Could he be one hundred percent positive that he had in fact met up with the SEALs? That first encounter with one of the zombies, not thirty minutes after landing, seemed like something out of a sci-fi movie. Things like that don't happen. It made sense that he'd dreamt it. He'd heard of that kind of thing happening before to people under sedative and heavy pain killers, both of which had been in his system. Morphine dreams, he'd heard the phenomenon called. Men would recall vivid encounters with everything from women to aliens to sea creatures. Zombies were within the realm of possibility when they were imagined.

"Like I said, Sean, there is no record of a Charles Turksen ever serving in the U.S. Navy. And most certainly not as a SEAL."

Sean nodded, though he didn't know what to believe at that point. "I," he paused a beat, "I don't know what happened."

Kemp placed his hand on Sean's shoulder. "It's okay, Sean. You've been through a traumatic event. The kind that can cause a man to doubt many things in his life." Kemp straightened, his face became solemn again. "Someone will be by your home when you get settled back in the U.S. They'll show you photographs of the area. In part to see what you might remember. You know, little details that might come back over time. They'll also show you where you were found, your condition, and what happened after you were rescued. If you wish to see it, that is."

"Okay," Sean said.

"You are a lucky man, Sean. You're the only one that survived. Someone, or something was on your side that night."

He doubted it. "Anything else?"

Kemp looked over his shoulder and nodded. The man on the right side of the door stepped forward and handed him a folder. Kemp opened it and laid it on Sean's lap.

"What's this?"

"Discharge papers and information on how your settlement will work, future benefits, things like that. The government is going to take care of you, Sean. In a few days you'll have enough money in your bank account that you'll never have to worry about bills, and college for your daughter, and all of the other little financial stresses ever again. You'll also continue to receive a check in the amount of your current pay, plus full benefits for you and your family, for life. And the prosthetic procedure is on the government as well." Kemp turned and started toward the door. He stopped and spun around. "There's a number on the last page in that folder, Sean. If you're ever unsure about what happened, or you think you're going to discuss those crazy dreams, you call that number and speak to the man who answers. He'll be able to help you."

Sean flipped to the last page in the folder and saw a ten digit number scribbled on a piece of yellow legal paper. There was no name or anything else written on the page, only the number. "Who'll answer?" he asked without looking up.

There was no reply.

Sean lifted his eyes and scanned the room. The men had left, the room was empty. He leaned back into his pillow and allowed his mind to replay events that he thought had happened in Nigeria. Each time he watched a scene play out, it seemed more surreal than it previously had. He accepted the fact that Kemp had been right. The events took place in his head, not real life. He needed that to be the truth.

Sean looked over at the half empty tray of food next to his bed. His stomach growled in response, but he didn't have the desire to eat at that moment. Instead, he closed his eyes and decided to get some sleep. It was not to happen, though.

Someone knocked on the door.

"Mr. Ryder? I hope I'm not disturbing."

Chapter 21

"I'm Dr. Kaufmann," the bearded man said with a thick German accent. He approached Sean's bed and extended his hand. Sean took it while he studied the weathered face in front of him. The doctor's hair was white with a few speckles of black. His blue eyes stood out against his red nose and cheeks. "I'm going to give you a new leg, Sean. A leg, which while it'll be made from titanium, will organically bond with your femur bone. You, like almost all of my patients, will find that you have feeling and sensation in your artificial limb."

Sean raised a curious eyebrow, which was met with a smile by the doctor.

"I know," Kaufmann said. "It sounds crazy."

"You have no idea," Sean said, smiling.

"This discovery was quite the shock to us all when my first patient recounted being able to feel the ground beneath a foot that had been dust for over twenty years. What I do, well, it's called an osseointegrated titanium implant. The short of it is that there will be direct contact between the titanium implant and the bone. You can look at it like I fuse them together, and then the bone bonds with the titanium, sort of growing into it. The long of it—"

"I don't want to know the long of it, Doc."

"Fair enough," Dr. Kaufmann said. Sean presumed the disappointed look on the man's face was because he wouldn't get to share the science behind the procedure. "Basically, the attached implant will end where your knee had existed. You'll have two titanium leg attachments that will connect with the permanent prosthesis, forming a joint. One will give you a full range of movement and will be better for everyday activities. The other is specially designed for running. Despite the prosthesis being in two pieces, most of my patients say they can feel their entire leg, and even the sensation of stepping on the ground. They feel the soles of their feet and can even replicate the feeling of wiggling their toes. Some can feel cold and hot through their new legs. Best of all, no one will be able to tell you have a prosthetic leg if you are wearing long pants. You might have a slight limp, but surely nothing that says, *hey this guy has a fake leg.*"

There was something about the doctor that led Sean to feel like he could trust the man. Perhaps it was his smile, or maybe his jovial face. Regardless, Sean knew that he'd let the man operate on him. "When can you perform the surgery?"

"I inspected your leg this morning, and it looks like we can get to it immediately. The freshness of the wound makes a few things easier, and a few things more difficult. In the end, it will play no role in your rehabilitation."

"What about the rehab?" Sean asked.

"You'll be here about four weeks, Sean. One for rest, three for rehabilitation, then you'll be on your way home. Any other questions?"

Sean shook his head and said nothing.

"Very well, then. The nurses will be in early to prep you. The next time you see me, you'll have a brand new leg."

Sean hadn't gotten used to the idea of having no leg yet, so having a brand new one seemed more exciting to the doctor than to himself. He smiled anyway and thanked the man.

Sleep came fast, thanks to the drugs the nurse gave him after Dr. Kaufmann left. He was restless though, as visions of the facility in Nigeria plagued him, both in his sleep and the waking states in between. What was truth and what was fiction? The lines were blurred. The problem was that he could see the events with such clarity. The eyes of the woman in the hall hovered above him, staring down at him with that pleading gaze, begging him to put an end to her misery. Nonsense, he told himself. Those visions were the things of science fiction and there was no way any of that had happened. He had to accept the account provided by Kemp. There was no other logical explanation. Except when it came to Turk. He'd known Turk almost as long as he'd been a PJ. They'd served side by side on several rescue and recovery missions. Dreams could not have provided him with so many past memories.

Could they?

Two nurses entered the room at six a.m. He was wide awake and greeted them with a smile. They wheeled Sean into a room for surgery prep where he was given a brief explanation of what would happen throughout the day. He paid little attention to them, feeling that he knew all he needed to know. He was getting a new leg, plain and simple.

They anesthetized him prior to taking him to the operating room. Moments before fading into a deep sleep, Sean wondered if they'd told his wife that he wouldn't be joining her for breakfast.

When Sean came to, his leg hurt like hell. Almost as bad as having his femur sawed through. He grimaced and blinked his eyes open. It took several attempts to clear his vision. He heard voices in the room. They started off sounding muffled, like he was underwater and someone was trying to talk to him. After a moment, his ears cleared and he made out the sound of his wife talking to someone with a German accent. Sean turned his head. His wife and daughter were on one side of the bed, Dr. Kaufmann on the other.

"Welcome back, Sean," Kaufmann said. "I was telling your wife how successful the surgery was."

Sean's throat felt dry and scratchy, he nodded his response.

"You'll need to rest for a week," Kaufmann said. "Then we'll begin your rehabilitation."

A week turned into two, which turned into a month. Before he knew it, Sean was back home with Kathy and Emma. Together, they settled into a life that held little resemblance to the life he'd led as a PJ.

Chapter 22

Sean swung his legs over the edge of his bed and reached down with his hand until he found his everyday use titanium prosthetic foot and leg. His eyes scanned his nightstand and settled in on his digital alarm clock. Eleven a.m. "Christ," he muttered, as he attached his prosthesis to the permanent titanium rod that had bonded with his femur years earlier. He still remarked that what the doctor had told him all those years ago had come true. He had almost all of the same sensations with his titanium leg as the one made of flesh and bone that he had lost in Nigeria. He could even feel the ground beneath his feet, and could tell when he moved from soft to hard ground. A cold tile floor could send chills up his leg and throughout his entire body. A walk through hot sand registered with both his left foot and right foot equally, and he'd find himself scurrying to get to a spot where the beach was damp.

The first year home had been rough. Sean missed the action and excitement of his job, as well as the camaraderie he shared with his fellow PJs and other members of the Special Forces community. But that had been the easy part to manage.

The nightmares that centered on the facility and the distraught beings inside persisted five to six nights a week. Sean slept very little during that first year, and he became so belligerent that Kathy threatened to take Emma and leave. That prompted him to dial the number on the otherwise blank yellow paper he'd received in the German hospital, stuck in the back of his retirement folder. He had no idea who the man was that answered, only that he helped Sean in a way that he imagined no counselor could. He told the man everything he remembered about the facility. Over time, the nightmares subsided, until he had them once or twice a month at most. These days, the dreams occurred less often, and Sean had almost accepted as fact that he'd stepped on an IED.

But doubts had lingered. Enough so that Sean devoted a portion of the money the government had given him to building a twelve hundred square foot bunker under the house they bought in the mountains of southeastern Virginia, south of Roanoke, fifteen miles or so east of I-81.

He and Kathy had fought over moving at first. They had a home and friends in Virginia Beach. She had a life there. But Sean's life there was dead. All he saw were memories of Jules. No matter how convincing they'd been in telling him that Jules death had been a result of an explosion, Sean could never shake a recurring vision of him aiming a gun at Jules and pulling the trigger.

Kathy agreed to move, and they settled into their new environment. She found work in the city, and Sean caught on as a volunteer with the Fire Department. Two or three days a week he would hang out at the firehouse and help clean the trucks, store gear and help with general repairs. When there was a call, he'd ride with the firefighters and assist in various ways depending on the situation. His training as a PJ prepared him for almost anything, and they found him an asset to have around.

Sean made his way down the stairs and into the kitchen. He poured a cup of warm coffee and scrambled a few eggs for breakfast. Before he could sit down to eat, his cell phone rang. He glanced at the screen and saw that it was Kathy calling.

"Hey, Babe," Sean said. "How's Seattle?"

"I got a line-up of conferences you wouldn't believe," she said.

"You're probably right," he said, hoping that she wouldn't go into detail.

Kathy laughed. "Did Emma get off to school okay?"

Sean glanced toward the front door and saw that his daughter's backpack was not hanging from its hook. He didn't want to admit that he had slept past his alarm and missed his daughter leaving for the bus. "Yeah, she's at school."

"Okay. Well, three days then I'm back home. Think you can handle it?"

"The fridge is stocked with frozen dinners," Sean said. "I think we're good."

"You sure? I could always get Barb to come over and make a meal for you."

Barb was short for Barbara Whaley, Kathy's best friend. The woman was single and forty and attractive. She spent most weekend nights at Sean's house, hanging out with him and his wife.

"Nah," Sean said. "I don't want to be a hassle. We'll be okay."

They finished their conversation then Sean returned to his breakfast, deciding to move into the living room so he could watch TV. He flipped through the local channels with the sound muted. It didn't take him long to realize that something had happened. Every station was broadcasting a news report thirty minutes too early. He set his fork on the plate of half-eaten eggs and got up as he unmuted the television.

"Officials are saying that the pandemic is confined at this time. There have been no reports in the U.S. as of yet," the woman said. "Travel to and from the following regions has been restricted." The reporter went on to list most of Africa, the Middle East and western Asia. The picture changed to still images of sick people in third world countries. "Signs include flu like symptoms: fever, aches and pains, chills, hot flashes, nausea," the list went on and Sean knew every symptom before the woman said it.

Sean rubbed his eyes, not sure he was really seeing what was being shown on TV. He hustled to the kitchen and grabbed his cell phone. He pulled up Kathy's number and was about to call her when the reporter said something that caught his eye.

"We're getting a report from Tangier, Morocco, of..." The reporter's face went white. "I... Cut to the tape."

A live feed took over the screen. It blinked and froze every few seconds like it was being broadcast via cell phone or webcam. Despite the bad feed, Sean made out the bodies of the afflicted as they shuffled through the dirty city street. At times, four or five of them would converge on someone too stupid to stay out of their way. They'd tear the person apart, limb by limb, and feast on the body.

Sean's phone rang. He muted the TV and answered without looking at the caller ID.

"Babe," he said. "You watching this?"

"I'm not your babe."

He recognized the voice. It was dark and deep and commanding.

"But I take it you're watching the same thing I am."

"Yeah," Sean said. "Who is this?"

"You know who this is."

"I know it sounds a lot like someone I was told didn't exist." Sean rose. "And if that someone did exist, and they stayed away from me for eight years while I fought daily to convince myself that I wasn't fucking insane, well, then that someone better stay far away from me. I may be missing a leg, but I can still kick anyone's ass. I'm stocked with weapons and have no reservations about using them."

"Good, you're going to need to." There was a pause. The man continued. "I'm sorry about that, Sean. They told me that if I reached out to you, they'd take my family. After twenty years as a SEAL, they had a lot on me. What was I to do? Look, Ryder, that shit we saw was real. I knew it was only a matter of time before those *things* made it far enough for it to turn into a pandemic. Now it's happened. That's why I'm reaching out to you. Do you hear me, Sean? The friggin' apocalypse is here."

Sean fell onto his couch. Could this really be happening?

"You there, Ryder?"

"Where are you, Turk?"

"Near Charleston, South Carolina. I got a set up here, a bunker and a compound. It's all heavily fortified. I got a select group of people that will be staying here. Some family, a couple guys from the old SEAL team and their families. I want you to come out here. Bring your family. The way I see it, we've got about twelve hours before breakouts start happening in the U.S. That's when all hell will break loose."

Sean felt his head spin. Two versions of reality competed for space in his brain. The nightmares and images that he'd fought so hard to repress were now the truth that he had to accept and recall in frightening detail. But first he had to organize his family and his things if they were going to make it to Charleston in time.

"Where are you, Sean?" Turk asked.

"Near Roanoke, Virginia."

"So about six hours. You need to get moving now. Roads are going to start getting clogged as word of this gets out."

"Kathy's across the country. She's in Seattle. I can't leave without her."

"Shit," Turk said. "See if you can get her on a plane to Charleston. I can have someone meet her at the airport and bring her here. Will that work?"

"Yeah," Sean said.

"Okay." Turk gave Sean coordinates to the location of the compound. "And look, Sean, if things go south, you go underground and you stay there for at least three weeks. That's the minimum. You got somewhere you can go?"

"Yeah, I built a place here on my land. It's stocked. We can survive there for months." He walked to the window and parted the blinds with this thumb and forefinger. "Turk, why three weeks?"

"I figure that's about the global lifespan of this virus. After that it blows itself out. But, as you probably remember, it can be transferred through bodily fluids. So once you come out, you be careful."

"How do you know this?"

"The tunnel."

"Say again?"

"When I was helping you out of that hell hole, we had to go through this long ass tunnel. I kept you talking. You told me everything some scientist named Knapp told you."

"Knapp," Sean repeated. It started to come back to him.

"I got other people to call, Sean. You're the first one I reached out to. Get moving."

"Okay," Sean said.

He hung up the phone, rose, opened the front door, grabbed his keys and walked out to his truck.

By the time he reached his daughter's school, the parking lot was full of concerned parents. He hopped the curb and parked in the grass, making sure to leave himself a way out should others do the same.

He pulled out his cell and dialed Kathy's number. The call went to voicemail.

"Hey, Babe," he said. "I know you're in a meeting now, but once you get this message I want you to head straight to the airport and get on a plane to Charleston, South Carolina, okay? Don't come home. Don't wait for anyone. Don't tell anyone what you're doing. Don't even go back to your hotel. Straight to the airport, Kathy. Call me as soon as you have your flight information."

He hung up and stuffed the phone in his pocket. He worried that the tone of his message might frighten his wife, and wondered if he should call her back and leave a more reassuring message for her.

"Dad," he heard Emma yelling.

He scanned the mass of people crowded around the school's entrance and saw his daughter heading toward him. Sean rounded the front of his truck and opened the passenger door for her.

As he ushered her in, she asked, "What's going on, Dad?"

Sean slammed her door, cut across the front of the truck and hopped in behind the wheel.

"Dad?"

He turned his head and looked his daughter in the eye. He reached for her hand, held it firmly in his.

"The apocalypse."

Affliction Z continues in Book 2. Anticipated release date: Early May, 2013.

Sign up for L.T. Ryan's *Affliction Z* new release newsletter and be the first to find out when new the next story is published. All new releases are discounted the first 48 hours. To sign up, simply fill out the form on the following page:

http://afflictionz.com/newsletter/

Click here to like Affliction Z on facebook.

Author's Note and About Affliction Z

Thank you for reading my book, Affliction Z: Patient Zero. I hope you enjoyed the story and are excited for Book 2! Here's a little of what you can expect...

I currently have four books planned in the Affliction Z series. That could be expanded depending on how the events of each novel unfold. Patient Zero (book 1) was originally not intended to be its own novel. It was supposed to be roughly 50 pages, but grew to four times that amount. As I got into the story, the events unfolded in such as way that it became apparent that it deserved to be its own book in the series.

In addition to the series, I have a stand-alone novel that takes place in the Affliction Z post-apocalyptic world. I'll also be releasing short stories and novellas based on the events in the series. These shorter works will be based on secondary characters and events that may or may not be mentioned in the series books. The first shorter work will be titled, The Sickness of Ronald Winters. I do plan on offering it as a free download for newsletter subscribers, so make sure you sign up by visiting the link above.

The current plan is for the books to be released in the following order:

Affliction Z: Patient Zero (book 1) - March, 2013
Affliction Z: BOOK 2 - May, 2013
The Sickness of Ronald Winters - June, 2013
Affliction Z: BOOK 3 - Late Summer/Fall, 2013

Affliction Z: BOOK 4 - TBD
Stand-Alone Novel - TBD

I also write an Action/Suspense Thriller series based on a character named Jack Noble. If you enjoy characters like Jason Bourne, Jack Bauer, Jack Reacher, etc., then have a look at the books below.

Lee "L.T." Ryan

Other Books by L.T. Ryan

Noble Intentions: Season One

Jack Noble. Assassin for hire. Spy. Thief. He makes no mistakes. Passes no judgement. Feels no remorse. So why does he stop to help a lost child moments before he's supposed to complete a deal with one of the east coast's top crime bosses?

A simple decision that places Jack in unfamiliar territory. He's become the hunted and finds himself in a race against time to save those closest to him.

Noble Intentions: Season One is a fast-paced, thrilling and suspenseful story of underworld crime and government secrets.

http://www.amazon.com/Noble-Intentions-Season-Episodes-ebook/dp/B0092ETUTC

Noble Intentions: Season Two

Season Two picks up where Season One left off. Jack Noble is dead. That's what the world believes, at least. Truth is, he's been laying low on the Greek island of Crete. Six months have passed, and with them, so has Jack's edge. But then he gets the call and it's time to return to action. Jack made a mess, and now is the time to clean it up. One way or another, he's determined to repay his debt. But will it cost him his life?

http://www.amazon.com/Noble-Intentions-Season-Episodes-ebook/dp/B00AVMTF8U/

Noble Beginnings: A Jack Noble Novel

In March of 2002, while the eyes of the world focused on Afghanistan, Jack Noble finds himself on the outskirts of Baghdad, Iraq. A Marine in name only, Jack is on-loan to the CIA. Normally an integral part of the team, he finds that he is nothing more than a security detail in Iraq.

Jack and his partner Bear have a run-in with four CIA special agents over the treatment of an Iraqi family. Within hours Jack and Bear are detained.

All Jack wanted was to finish his enlistment and move on with his life. All he did was intervene and save a family from unwarranted violence at the hands of four CIA agents. But he soon discovers that he did far more than intervene. He has placed himself dead square in the middle of a conspiracy that reaches the highest levels of the U.S. government.

http://www.amazon.com/Noble-Beginnings-Jack-Novel-ebook/dp/B009K8RHNQ

A Deadly Distance (Jack Noble #2)

Washington, D.C. Midday. A man waits at a bus stop, his intentions unknown. Two government operatives have been stalking him for days, waiting for him to make his move. Unexpectedly, the man takes off running and heads for a deserted warehouse.

Jack Noble and his partner, Frank Skinner, believe the man to be part of a terrorist organization that is involved in smuggling drugs and guns and men into the country. But it turns out their plan involves far more export than import, and hits a lot closer to home.

As the case unfolds, the man behind it all reaches out to Jack with a simple message... 37 hours.

Made in the USA
Monee, IL
26 July 2023

39946034R00097